I0703066

AUCTIONED TO THE VAMPIRE

Copyright © 2024 by Entice Publishing LLC
www.RosalynStirling.com

Auctioned to the Vampire
The Wild Shadows, #0.5

All rights reserved. No parts of the book may be used or reproduced, transmitted, stored in, or introduced into a retrieval system in any form or by any means (including but not limited to electronic, mechanical, photocopying, and recording) without written permission from the author or publisher nor otherwise circulated in any form of binding or cover other than that in which it is published without a similar condition being imposed on the subsequent purchaser. The exception is for the use of brief quotations in a book review.

This book is a work of fiction. Names, characters, establishments, organizations, and incidents are either products of the author's imagination or are used fictitiously to give a sense of authenticity. Any resemblance to actual persons, living or dead, events, or locales is entirely coincidental.

To all the readers who are tired of the virgin trope.
Unless he's the virgin.
I see you.

Trigger Warnings

This novel contains mature elements and themes, including (but not limited to) explicit sexual content, violence, death, sexual assault, references to an abusive romantic relationship (financial abuse and sexual coercion, referenced/off the page), abusive parent relationship (referenced/off the page), mention of rape (referenced/off the page), human/vampire trafficking, and sexual slavery. Reader discretion is advised.

Chapter One

ROWAN

Few can resist the allure of a vampire bite.

Fewer still can resist a virgin vampire on sale in the underground market. And Rowan knew the moment they arrived at the remote village of Shadowbank that he was running out of time.

"Let's go, boy," hissed Jonas, the ringleader of their traveling troupe.

Silver chains clanked at Rowan's wrists as Jonas hauled him from where he'd been chained inside the barred carriage. The fading light of the afternoon sun met his eyes that had become too accustomed to complete darkness. For days, he'd been forced to crouch beneath a thick blanket, hiding the glow of his body and thus the very essence of what he was.

A vampire.

His kind wasn't welcome in many human villages. He doubted this one would be any different. It was why he hadn't been able to run even if he wanted to. There was nowhere to run to—not in these remote lands with only hostile human settlements and a massive forest filled with demons and other creatures of the dark.

All around him, performers and other members of their traveling troupe shouted, hauling boxes from the backs of wagons or bringing horses into nearby stables. The streets had the usual afternoon bustle of villagers moving about their business or finishing up work for the day and heading home or to taverns and brothels. Shadowbank appeared like every other remote village they'd traveled to—filled with a few hundred people that were harder than the land they refused to leave. The land with death hovering a breath away.

There was another yank at his chains, and pain sliced through every inch of skin exposed to the metal. His stomach turned as he bit back a hiss threatening to escape through his teeth. He stumbled out of the barred carriage, barely catching himself before he sprawled face-first on the cobblestone street.

The shackles on his wrists were connected to a chain that led to the shackles on his ankles. A second chain went from his wrists to the silver collar around his neck. Beneath the collar and shackles, his skin was blistered and red despite his vampire abilities to heal quickly.

His fangs sunk into his lower lip as the need to feed swelled inside of him. The sound of every heartbeat of the traveling troupe around him thrummed loudly in his ears. Performers strode by, carrying boxes, satchels, costumes, and props toward a large stone building with a sign hanging above the door.

The House of Obscurities.

The place he would soon be sold.

In some places, vampires were looked upon as the predators they were. They roamed freely and fed upon willing—and unwilling—mortals. In other places with far more wealth, the humans were armed with silver-tipped arrows or spears and refused to allow vampires entry. But in the rare instances where humans captured vampires with the silver that weakens them, they were some of the most prized possessions in underground auctions.

Grunting, he bit back the pain as the silver pressed into his already raw flesh, but he said nothing as the ringleader continued hissing obscenities at him. As if Rowan had done anything except obey Jonas' every command without objection for months.

The ringleader looked around the darkening streets.

Rowan knew Jonas was ensuring there were no enchantresses around—the female magic wielders who protected human villages and cities and were law unto themselves. The sale of any of the races was forbidden, even one so disliked as the vampires.

Suddenly, there was a drop of weight from around his neck, and he glanced down. His necklace had fallen to the ground, and he quickly reached for it. As he did, Jonas jerked his chains.

"Leave it," the ringleader hissed. "Why do you insist on keeping that thing?"

Rowan grabbed the necklace—a simple leather chain with a roughly cut emerald pendant—before Jonas was pulling him across the street.

"The first person I bed will receive this necklace," he said, recalling the precious little he knew of his father's culture—the man who'd been too drunk to do more than collect debt. "Surely, it's something you'd be sympathetic toward, given why I'm here."

Jonas muttered but didn't object as Rowan tied the necklace back around his neck, his chains rattling all the while.

Rowan passed dozens of performers and the troupe's many vampire guards as he was pulled through the back door by Jonas, who gripped his chains in gloved hands. No one bothered to stand up for him. Instead, they looked the other way, eyes too focused on other tasks.

Like Rowan, most weren't there of their own volition. Many had made deals with Jonas to get out of their home villages and acquire safety along the demon-infested roads. Travel in these remote territories was too dangerous otherwise.

Rowan was too valuable to risk standing up for, anyway.

Unlike the other members of Jonas' traveling troupe, Rowan was the only one who was shackled—human, vampire, or otherwise. And with the added misfortune of being a virgin. Not only would his bite be more alluring than the average vampire since he was a fledgling, but his body would have its own appeal. With his skin that glowed when touched by the light of the moon, many would pay for the chance to use his body and fangs. As soon as they took his virginity, he would no longer glow. But his bite... that would hold a great appeal for many months yet.

Rowan strode down several flights of warped, wooden stairs by the lights of lanterns into a hidden underground room with a bar to one side and a circular, wooden stage at the center of the room. Around it, there were rows of benches and large chairs for the wealthy to make their bids on the *goods* presented to them.

At the center of the stage were eight women, all dressed in simple but elegant red gowns that were low cut—and bared their necks.

Swallowing thickly, his fangs sunk further into his lips. He tasted blood, which made his hunger spike further. At the sight of the human women, his cock hardened, and he placed his hands over his crotch as he was pulled onto the stage by his chains.

His eyes settled on a woman with hair the color of flames. Her ringlets hung down to her mid back, and she had skin as beautiful and fair as freshly fallen snow. Countless freckles dusted her nose and cheeks. But more alluring than her hair was the look of fiery determination in her eyes, and he couldn't help but notice the way she fisted her hands at her side.

"Welcome back, Jonas," said a tall woman with dark brown hair and a black dress with lace that covered her chest and neck. "I've made the preparations as you requested." She gestured to the women in red dresses. "Should any of them come to harm, this will be the last time you and your troupe will be permitted here."

The implication—both spoken and unspoken—behind her words was clear.

Feed too much, and the enchantresses would know Jonas had brought vampires inside the village's wall—and kick them out. And if Jonas had any hope of keeping the presence of vampires a secret, they needed humans who could remain quiet after being fed on.

Jonas released Rowan's chains, and Rowan nearly sagged with relief at the lack of pressure at the back of his neck. He could feel his skin blistering, popping, and attempting to heal only to redden and burn again at the touch of silver. Biting back the pain, he pushed his dark hair back, rattling the chains as he did.

"Madam Trista," Jonas said with his arms wide. His tone implied mock surprise as he held a hand to his chest. "You wound me. I would never jeopardize our relationship. It will be as you say."

The ringleader appeared to be a man in his forties. He was of a height with Rowan, but he was far wider and a solid wall of muscle. But he was no mortal. Like his guards, he was a vampire who had to keep his identity a secret to travel inside human settlements. And he wore gloves, careful to avoid touching Rowan's silver chains.

Jonas gestured to Rowan. "Of course, the star of the show must be seen to first. He has a big night ahead tomorrow. Can't have him scaring off the clientele."

Eating the clientele, Rowan thought.

The madam's eyes narrowed, and her lips thinned.

"Besides," Jonas continued in a quieter tone laced with the menace Rowan knew too well. "Without me, your little brothel would be out of business. So few journey to Shadowbank these days with the demons amassing in numbers."

Rowan hadn't been able to see much beneath the blanket in his cage as they'd traveled, but he had heard the roar of demons and hissing of creatures of the dark during many of the nights when they set up camp. The closer they'd come to Shadowbank and the forest, the worse and more frequent the attacks became. Without the vampire guards, none of them would have survived.

Trista's eyes narrowed as her hands settled on the shoulders of the woman with red hair. "If you disrespect me in my house again, I'll hand you over to the enchantresses—money or not."

"I meant no disrespect," Jonas said, head bowing slightly. Then he tossed a massive bag of coins over to Trista, which she caught. "Let's proceed."

There was a hand behind Rowan's back as he was shoved forward—toward the women. His chains rattled as their gazes settled upon him. Rather than those eyes feeling like a weight on his shoulders, it felt like the still air before the storm. The nervous tension in the room from these females left a strange buzzing in the air.

I was like you, he thought toward them. *I won't hurt you.*

At least, he'd try not to. He'd been turned only months ago and had little experience in controlling his hunger.

Taking a breath to steady himself, he scanned the eight women garbed in dresses the color of blood. It was a strategic choice—likely intended to disguise any signs of spilled blood. But he had eyes only for the woman at the center. The one with hair even brighter than her gown. She was slim of frame with narrow hips and thin limbs, and he thought to wonder whether she'd eaten that morning.

She looks like I did before my father sold me, he thought. But his father received fewer coins than those Trista had been given. His life had been worth so little.

Soon, he'd be sold to whatever mortal wished to use him for his fangs and his cock. And then he'd have even fewer choices than he did now.

Seeing Rowan's eyes settle on the woman with red hair, the madam said, "This is Nemera."

The woman stepped toward him, her dark eyes fixing on his as though she couldn't even see his chains. Her eyes were as round and soft as her face, and he saw no disgust there. Instead, a hint of curiosity seemed to flicker in the back of her gaze. Was that resignation as well? Surely not. Mortals longed for the bite of a vampire and the pleasure it brought.

She brushed her thick red curls over a shoulder, baring her neck to him.

"Take what you need."

Her voice was like the steady rainfall of spring—infused with hope and new life.

I shouldn't touch her, he thought, still loathing his need for mortal blood. His fangs lengthened further, and he could feel his lips peeling back. Reminding himself she'd agreed to this and was accepting payment, he took a step forward and then another. His chains rattled, the shackles burning his wrists.

When she was only a step away, his eyes focused on the faint pulsing in her neck. The blood moving through her veins. He longed to reach out and wrap his arms around her. Instead, he left his chained hands in front of his hardened cock and leaned forward.

Then he sunk his fangs into her.

NEMERA'S HEART drummed a nervous beat in her chest as the vampire drank from her.

He was the most handsome male she had ever seen. He was tall and fair of skin. Although he wasn't as broad as the farmers and other laborers in town, muscles corded his arms, complementing his lean frame. But in his eyes, a darkness lingered.

What am I doing? Surely, I must have a death wish, she thought.

It was far too late to go back now. She'd volunteered. The money she'd get from this was more than she'd make in a month upstairs at the bar. There was no way she'd say no—not after her ex-husband had left her without a home or a single coin to her name.

As the vampire pulled draft after draft of her life's blood into him, her hands found his black shirt, which was simple but made of fine material.

Vampire bites aren't like what everyone says, she thought, surprised not to feel a surge of desire. Outside of wanting to feel his body pressed against hers, she didn't feel anything toward this male. What she did feel was simply because she found him handsome. Devastatingly so.

Maybe the venom didn't affect her like it did others.

Suddenly, something tingled at her neck where his teeth sunk into her, followed by a feeling of warmth fluttering through her veins.

Then desire crashed over her like the ocean's oncoming tide.

At that moment, she wanted nothing more than to rip this male's clothes off of him. It didn't matter that her friends and the madam were behind her nor that the ringleader and his bodyguards were at the base of the stairs to the stage. She knew that if this vampire had asked her to spread her legs, her response would have been, "How far?"

A moan threatened to escape her lips, and she sunk her teeth into her lower lip.

There was a brush of fingers against her stomach. Daring a glance down, she saw he'd fisted the red fabric of her dress in one of his shackled hands. Almost as though he desired her as much as she did him.

Stop it, some distant part of her thought. *Remember what happened last time.*

She'd thought she'd been following her heart—marrying a man her family had chosen for her. She'd been young and foolish enough to think he loved her, too. How naïve she'd been, so easy to manipulate. As she'd come to learn, he'd just wanted something from her. And it was because of him she'd lost everything.

As the vampire drank from her, he wedged one of his legs between hers, and she let him. Unbidden, her hips moved against his thigh, and she could feel herself growing wet. If he didn't stop soon, she'd be coming—in front of everyone. Pleasure swelled within her, and her fingers tangled in his shirt, desperate to feel his body pressed against hers. She wanted, no she *needed,* to feel his skin on hers.

For the first time, she understood the stories about vampires

—and why so many women of the village had openly said they'd bed one if the opportunity ever presented itself.

Suddenly, he moved, his fangs pulling free. She gasped, a little whimper escaping her lips. But the male didn't put space between them. Instead, he wrapped his lips over where his fangs had been, running his tongue over the sensitive flesh. Even without him feeding on her, molten desire spiked in her core. Again, her hips thrust against his leg.

Her breaths became shallow, and she suspected he could hear his effect on her with his sharp senses—or perhaps even smell her desire. But she could have sworn she heard his breaths grow ragged as he held on to her dress between his fingers. As if he wanted more, too.

"That's enough," came a male voice before the handsome vampire stepped back.

It was the ringleader. But she didn't have eyes for him. Instead, her gaze fixed on the eyes of the vampire before her.

"What's your name?" she asked, suddenly desperate to have some piece of this male who she'd likely never see again.

She was rarely allowed in the basement after all.

But the male didn't speak. Instead, he was forcefully turned away from her, and it was then she noticed the redness of the skin on his neck and wrists.

Silver, she realized. *Here I was thinking about my selfish desires when this male is not just hungry but in pain—tortured.*

Why? Was he violent to the others in the troupe and needed to be restrained? But then why did the ringleader call him the star of the show?

She watched from the stage as he was dragged across the room and into an adjoining hallway before disappearing.

At that moment, she knew one thing with certainty.

She had to see him again.

Chapter Two

NEMERA

Hours later, night had fallen, and the worn faces of villagers started to fill the common room of the House of Obscurities.

Nemera walked behind the bar, filling a few tankards and passing them out to patrons and taking their coins. Pausing, she tightened the scarf around her neck, careful that her bite marks weren't seen.

"Did you hear what happened in the fields?" one patron whispered to the man beside him at the corner of the bar. Both were corded with muscles—likely laborers at the docks by the look of their worn leather clothes.

"Aye," replied the other man. "A fengrine attack. Didn't they all die?"

There had been another demon attack on the fields at the eastern edge of the town that were outside of the ward—this time by the wolf-like creatures the size of two carriages stacked with multiple rows of sharp teeth. They were fast, and they were deadly. Few humans who saw the fengrine ever lived to tell the tale.

"All except one was killed," the first man said. "From the

sounds of it, the lad barely made it through the ward before the demons were upon it."

"Thank fuck at least he made it," the first male rasped before tilting his head back and swallowing the rest of his drink. "We'd all be dead without the ward. But the enchantresses need to expand it so it covers the fields."

The man shifted, and his gaze settled on Nemera. Blinking, she realized she'd been staring and shook herself. She grabbed his empty tankard without waiting for him to respond and refilled it.

The man was right. The ward surrounding the village was the only reason any of them could survive in a land so close to the forest and its demons. They were too far from the protection of the cities and their magic wielders. The only thing keeping the demons and creatures of the forest at bay was the ward.

But leaving Shadowbank and its ward was almost impossible.

Travel by the roads was too dangerous for humans like Nemera to dare to do on her own. Travel by boat, while somewhat safer, was far too expensive. The creatures of the deep didn't always venture to the surface and attack the ships leaving the harbor, but leaving by ship would cost a small fortune. Most would have to sell their homes to afford it.

The door to the brothel banged open and several enchantresses strode through, pushing their hoods back to reveal the fair faces of the most powerful magic wielders of Shadowbank.

So powerful they'd done nothing when I'd been destitute— without a home and forced to sleep in the streets, she thought. Bitterness rooted in her heart, but she was careful not to let it show on her face.

At the front was the second-in-command to the head enchantress, Arabella. Like her companions, she dressed in black leathers, from her tall laced boots to her pants, corset, and jacket. In her hair were silver chains with a single teardrop gemstone coming down to her forehead. She and her companions were heavily armed, and Arabella wore two swords at her back. She stood taller than many of the patrons and wore her long, dark hair in a single braid. Like the vampire, she was lean, and her limbs were corded with muscles.

Best not to think about him, Nemera thought.

Forcing a smile, she nodded to Arabella and her three companions as they strode over to the bar. The dock workers who'd been standing there moved aside, making space for the enchantresses.

"A round of drinks, please," said Jessamine, the blonde enchantress standing at Arabella's side. Jessamine was far shorter than Arabella and curvier as well.

Nemera nodded. "Of course."

A minute later, she'd filled four tankards and passed them to the enchantresses. Jessamine and the others headed for the tables, but Arabella lingered after paying.

"Was there something else?" Nemera asked.

While Arabella wasn't known to be cruel, she'd rarely spoken with Nemera directly outside of orders at the bar. But the enchantress hesitated, seeming to be deep in thought.

"I heard there's a troupe in town," Arabella said, leaning an arm on the bar. As she did, Nemera spotted several knives in hidden sheaths inside her jacket. "Are they staying here?"

Nemera's heartbeat immediately picked up, and she nodded carefully.

Had Arabella learned about the vampires already?

Trista had warned her that the enchantresses may come asking questions. She'd also said they couldn't speak a word of the vampires or what happened beneath the main floors of the brothel—whatever that business was. Nemera had never been allowed to go down there during the late hours when the secret patrons arrived. Trista had implied they'd be out of business if the enchantresses found out. And if Nemera had any hope of making enough money to start a new life, then she needed this job. So, she wasn't about to reveal anything to the enchantresses.

"Most of the troupe have taken rooms upstairs," Nemera said. "They'll perform later tonight and for the next few days."

On the public stage, she thought, careful to avoid mention of the basement.

Again, her thoughts drifted to the vampire and the feel of his lips against her neck.

"Were there any magic wielders among them?" Arabella pressed, her gaze sharp.

Brows furrowing, Nemera said, "Not that I noticed."

A strange question. Only vampires were forbidden from entering Shadowbank. Why would the enchantress be seeking other magic wielders?

Arabella licked her lips before standing upright and smoothing her jacket. She muttered something under her breath, and Nemera thought she heard the enchantress cursing, but she couldn't be sure over the noise of the common room. The music had stopped, replaced by the sounds of polite applause from their too-empty common room.

"Thanks," Arabella said before grabbing her drink and heading for the table with the other enchantresses.

Sighing, Nemera instinctively wiped the counter down with a cloth.

"Well done," Trista said, appearing beside her at the bar and watching as Arabella walked away.

"As I promised," Nemera said, thinking of the small coin purse stored in her room upstairs. The most coins she'd seen in one place since she'd been married. "I'll keep your confidence."

It had taken her months to get a job thanks to her ex-husband's gambling reputation. So many taverns and brothels wouldn't even let her pass through the front doors—spotting her bright red hair immediately—let alone ask for work. During that time, she'd slept in the streets. Trista had taken pity on her after she'd caught Nemera pulling stale bread from the trash outside the House of Obscurities. That was four years ago. It had taken Nemera this long to earn the madam's trust to even be told about the secret business in the basement, and she wasn't about to jeopardize it now.

Trista sighed, staring out at the common room, which would have been filled to bursting by this hour months ago.

"Do you want to revisit bartering?" Nemera asked, careful to keep her voice low as she wiped down the counter.

With fewer people coming into Shadowbank, commerce of any kind had been stilted. So few people had spare coin. Many had attempted to barter with the madam for access to the mistresses or sirs or for drinks. When it was made clear that only coins would be an acceptable form of payment, business had slowed significantly. No one could afford anything outside of essentials, let alone pleasures.

"No," Trista said simply. "Chickens and yarn won't pay for the oil to light this place or ale that fills tankards. Those are from just two businesses we frequent that only accept coin as payment. And so must we."

Nemera nodded. "Of course."

She didn't know anything about running a business. Who was she to question the madam's decision?

"That mind of yours is why I like you," Trista said, turning her gaze from the common room to look at Nemera. "It's also why I hired you all those years ago. You're not afraid to challenge what's been done."

Nemera blinked, uncertain what to say.

"But this is something we can't move on," Trista continued. "Or we'll be out of business before the next full moon."

"Is that why you're... hosting Jonas?" Nemera dared to ask.

Tolerating would be a better choice.

"The male is a necessary evil, like so many things out here," Trista said. "It's sink or swim. Live or die. Nothing else matters. You know this better than anyone."

Nemera licked suddenly dry lips.

Not wanting to think about the series of events that led her to a life where she worked herself ragged every single day without rest, she said, "Do you need any help with the troupe?"

She was careful to avoid mention of the basement and to speak low enough so no one nearby could hear.

Lines formed between Trista's brows. "Why?"

Shrugging, Nemera said, "It seems like things are set up here."

It was a lie, and they both knew it. Even with the slower business, there would always be patrons who needed refills or who ordered the stew of the day. There would always be spilled drinks to clean or rowdy customers to see to the door. But she had to see the vampire again, especially if the troupe would only be in town for a few days.

If she was being honest, she was also curious about the basement. Just what would happen while the ringleader and his troupe were here? What show was the vampire a part of?

Trista rolled her eyes, and the gesture had her looking far younger than her forty years. "You can't fuck him."

Blood rushed to Nemera's cheeks. "Who said anything about fucking anyone?"

Was it that obvious how the vampire affected her? But the thought of sharing her body with him had desire swirling in her core.

She hadn't slept with anyone since her husband—hadn't wanted to. But now? Well... It was like the vampire bite had awoken something inside of her. Something she'd thought long since dead.

Pausing, Trista looked around at the bar. No patrons were nearby at that moment, as most had shifted over to the seats surrounding the stage. Then she sighed and said, "You've done well today. If you'd like to work with our other patrons, I'll permit it this time. But be warned—Jonas is a cruel man."

Nemera stashed the cloth she'd been using to clean the counter and turned toward the doorway in the back and the staircase beyond. Before she could go, Trista caught her wrist.

Glancing up, Nemera thought she saw genuine concern in

Trista's eyes. "Be careful around the ringleader. And do not interfere with what happens below. For us to survive out here, it must remain."

Nemera hesitated.

What could be so bad that Trista felt the need to warn her in advance? Gooseflesh prickled along her skin.

"Yes, Madam."

Satisfied, Trista nodded, her eyes skirting down Nemera's sturdy boots, trousers, and apron. "Wear something nice. And keep your head down."

Without another word, Nemera turned and hurried to her room upstairs.

After her ex-husband had gambled away their home, she'd been forced to find another place to live. Trista had been the only one to offer her a place to rent—and work. Her ex-husband had burned so many bridges, and Nemera continued to shoulder the consequences of that.

Some days, looking at the patrons—her neighbors who hadn't helped her when she needed it the most—filled her with anger. It wasn't her fault that her husband had gambled and owed so many people money. He'd left her behind, fleeing their life and his debts, and her parents had disowned her when it was clear her husband no longer wanted her. So, how could the people she'd once thought of as friends not have possessed a shred of humanity to help her? Bitterness had rooted in her chest, making living in this village a hardship every day. It was a reminder of the lack of sympathy of others.

One day, she'd have enough money to afford her own home, and she'd never have to look to anyone for help ever again. She'd never rely on anyone but herself again. Not when all anyone else could do was hurt her if given the chance.

In her room, she changed into a long black dress that hugged her precious few curves. It was far from anything the mistresses and sirs wore during their rendezvous with clients, but it would have to do. Then she slipped on heeled boots and headed down hidden corridors in the back of the building toward the basement.

The same corridors she'd walked earlier that day before the vampire had fed on her.

When she came to a nondescript wooden door in the basement, a guard let her through without a word. Surprise hit her. Why hadn't he tried to stop her or asked who she was? Though she'd been working every day for months. Everyone likely knew her on sight. But this was only her second time down here. Perhaps once allowed in, the guards wouldn't stop her from coming again. As the thick door swung inward, she noted sound-proofing fabrics fastened to the inside as well as along the walls.

There was the distinct click of the door being locked behind her by a second guard.

The first thing she noticed was that the music was much quieter than the common room above. Several musicians played stringed instruments for the men and women dressed in far finer clothes than the patrons upstairs. They wore slacks and vests or gowns with lace gloves. Most were in dark colors. It was far easier to disguise their comings and goings in the late hours, she supposed.

There was a round stage at one end—directly beneath where the performers would be on the floor above—as well as a large bar where several dozen patrons stood, awaiting drinks. Unlike upstairs, there weren't barrels of ale. Instead, there were bottles of what Nemera knew was very expensive wine. The smell of wood polish hung in the air along with the sweeter scent of roses—quite unlike the smells of unwashed bodies and burned bread upstairs.

Not for the first time, she wondered why she was down here. Surely, it wasn't to see the vampire again. No, if she could prove she could be trusted working down here to Trista, she'd get new opportunities to make more money to afford her new life.

Taking a breath to steady her racing heart, she headed for the bar, joining the other staff there. This work was something she knew.

A strange hush settled over the room. It was as if everyone was waiting for something.

Glancing up, she noticed the ringleader emerge from a back room with his bodyguards at his heels. He wore long, black trousers and matching gloves and a jacket with long coattails. His brown hair was clean and slicked back. A few patrons approached him, speaking in hushed tones. He smiled and gestured to the corner of the room beyond the stage.

Slowly, her gaze shifted to where he'd indicated.

Her heart thudded as she spotted the vampire at the far end of the room, his chains hooked on to the wall and his hands over his head. Only now, he was shirtless. His chest was lean like the rest of him. Even from a distance, she could see the outlines of his abs. But far more stark were the burn marks in the exact shape of the chain links against his stomach.

Her insides twisted as something in her chest tightened.

This isn't right, she thought. *No one should be treated like this.*

The ringleader strode across the room and past dozens of onlookers in the seats surrounding the circular stage—a stage she'd stood on only hours ago with seven other women. Grabbing the vampire's chains, Jonas all but dragged him across the room before looping one of the chain's links between his hands and feet into a metal loop on the ground—trapping him at the center of the stage.

"Welcome, welcome," Jonas bellowed over the talking crowd.

The room immediately quieted. Those standing near the bar settled into open seats. Some even abandoned their drinks at the bar, forgetting them entirely. However, most were forced to stand in the back. There had to be at least fifty people there. Perhaps more.

"It's good to return to Shadowbank," Jonas said, addressing the crowd from where he stood on the stage. "It's been a few years, but this time, I've brought you a special treat." Turning, the ringleader made a sweeping motion and gestured to the vampire who stood shirtless at the center of the stage, his chest rising and falling in heaving breaths. "We all know the allure of the vampire bites. But what if I told you that not only could you be pleasured by fangs but by body as well? And you could train the vampire to your liking."

Nemera watched from her place behind the bar as several patrons' brows drew together, hungry gazes shifting between them.

"This isn't just any vampire," Jonas continued. Reaching back, he grabbed the male by his short black hair, pulling his head back—exposing his neck to the audience. It was then she noticed he wore an emerald necklace.

Nemera watched the movement of the vampire's throat as he swallowed, but he didn't fight the ringleader. Instead, the veins in his jaw bulged as though holding back a grunt of pain.

"I present to you," Jonas continued, "a virgin vampire."

The crowd gasped, and Nemera spotted a few gloved hands covering mouths. Some women fanned themselves, and not a few men's eyes narrowed in dark interest as though honing in on prey. Those men's looks could mean anything from eagerness for personal enjoyment to wanting their wives or lovers to be pleasured while they watched. Perhaps both.

"By the light of the moon, his skin glows, as does the skin of all virgin vampires," Jonas continued. "And can be yours to play with."

Fury bubbled up inside of Nemera like an oncoming thunderstorm.

This male was going to *auction* another living being? Sell him like he was nothing more than property?

Disgust filled her.

She'd witnessed firsthand the lack of humanity in this village. She shouldn't be surprised that people were capable of an even greater darkness. Had their proximity to the demons they feared brought out the worst in humanity? Or perhaps, even after everything, she still held on to the delusion that there was some semblance of goodness in others, that no one would willingly use another person for some type of gain, monetary or otherwise.

But there he was—a male she didn't know—being auctioned to a willing crowd.

She'd never hated another person. Not even her ex-husband. But something akin to hate swelled in her chest as she glared at Jonas.

Alongside the fury and disgust, another feeling swirled within her. It wasn't desire exactly. Could it be jealousy? But no, that was impossible. Anything she felt for the vampire was just from his bite. None of it meant anything.

Still, she found her gaze drawn to where the vampire held on to the chains, gripping them tightly in swiftly reddening hands as the ringleader released his hair.

Jonas pulled something from his jacket, which was adorned in golden embroidery. Her breath caught when she realized what it was.

A whip.

In a flash, the ringleader unfurled the leather whip, which was as long as the round stage. With a flick of his wrist, it slashed through the air with a booming *snap*. The audience gasped and those in the front row leaned back in their seats.

Only the vampire didn't move. Instead, his shoulders rounded as though he knew what was coming next.

There was another loud snap of the whip as leather connected with flesh. Veins bulged in the vampire's jaw as he clenched his teeth, but he didn't cry out when the whip connected against his bare back thrice more.

It was then that she realized she'd dropped both the glass she'd been cleaning and the rag atop the bar's counter. Tears welled at the corner of her eyes.

Stop it, she thought, her mind frantic. *Leave him alone.*

Once, she'd been a foolish woman with a big heart that her ex-husband had eagerly taken advantage of. Apparently, her heart hadn't hardened enough to the hardships of this world because tears streamed down her cheeks as she watched in horror, her hands clenched into fists.

Three more cracks of the whip and the audience was gasping and clapping hands, excited by this display of a docile vampire. Such a sight would make the male seem even more valuable. If he wouldn't lash out at a human when whipped, it likely meant he'd also be willing to obey other orders—that he could be *trained* as the ringleader had claimed.

It was likely why the ringleader was bothering to make this farce of a show—to drive up the prices.

She should close her eyes, should turn away.

If she had any hope of starting a new life, she had to keep her head down. She'd been working herself ragged for four years since she'd lost her home and the life she'd known. She couldn't risk losing everything she'd worked for—her job, her room, her new life—for another male. Especially not when she wasn't sure if she could get another job if she lost this one. Would she be sleeping in the streets again?

Like her ex-husband, this male would surely take advantage of her, too.

The sound of the whip cracked again.

Before she knew what she was doing, her feet were moving. She wove around the bar, past those standing at the back of the rings of seats, and to the stage, stopping directly before it.

"Sir," she began, her voice trembling faintly. She could feel every eye in the room settle on her, but she forced herself to ignore them. "The madam would like for you to share with the audience when our wonderful patrons can expect to... place their bids."

The words disgusted her, tasting bitter in her mouth. And it had nothing to do with the lie. If Trista learned of it, Nemera would deal with the consequences. But the idea of offering another living being to be sold—vampire or not—was despicable.

There was another snap of the whip before a gust of air slashed past her. She closed her eyes, waiting for the sting of the leather to kiss her skin, but it never came. There was a thud, and she opened her eyes to see the vampire had shifted his body so that he was between her and the ringleader, his shackles still locked onto the floor. The whip was wrapped around his forearm. Had he blocked the whip from hitting her?

Turning toward her, his blue eyes fixed on hers. His gaze made her feel like she'd been submerged under the ocean, powerful tides swirling around her, over her. Blue eyes had her rooted in place, and all sense of time lost meaning. Even with the coldness in his gaze, she felt herself longing to remain there, glimpsing pieces of his soul—feeling along the shards of memory and hope.

There was another snap of the whip, and the vampire's brows drew together as Jonas' whip cracked against his chest.

"That's enough," she said, finding her voice and glaring up at the ringleader. This time, there was no tremble in it.

Surely, this despicable man could see that—even having drank her blood—the wounds from the lashes weren't closing on the vampire's back and chest. He would be in genuine pain, and his hunger would increase, no doubt.

For the first time, she wondered how much the silver pressed against his skin weakened him. She doubted those shackles would be removed ever again if he was sold.

Unless I do something about it.

The ringleader's gaze fell on her, full of cold fury. Then the look was gone, replaced by an artificial smile as cold as the northern glaciers.

"Of course." Jonas rolled up the whip. Then he looked to the audience and said, "As you can see, I've brought to you a mild-tempered, virgin vampire that can be trained however you want—both in and out of the bedroom. He's newly turned and will have a bite even more seductive than a regular vampire bite. Return tomorrow night. Bidding will begin at midnight."

The audience clapped, but the sounds were strangely muted to her ears. Her throat tightened as the ringleader turned and descended the stage—heading right for her. Not bothering to slow his pace, his fingers closed around her arm painfully, and he pulled her toward the bar—the artificial smile never leaving his lips.

"Tell the madam if she or one of her girls ever interrupt me again," Jonas said, his eyes skirting around the room, likely looking for prying ears. "That I'll bring my merchandise to another establishment."

Nemera couldn't believe that Trista, the kind woman she had come to know, would allow auctions of this kind. Perhaps she was once again assuming the best in others when experience should have had her believing otherwise.

Hands clenched into fists, she said, "What makes you think she wouldn't report you to the enchantresses? You wouldn't get past the front doors before your *merchandise* was taken from you, and you and your men would be thrown into the prison cells."

Everyone knew of the dungeon deep beneath the stone fortress that the enchantresses called home. Few people were brought there so far as she knew, but he wouldn't know that.

I should report him, she thought, but immediately stopped that train of thought. If she told the enchantresses about the auctions, not only would Jonas be arrested, but so would Trista. Without the madam, all business would stop, and she'd lose her job—and once again be subject to life on the streets.

Eyes narrowing, Jonas closed the distance between them, smelling of sweat and too-sweet wine. Instinctively, she took a step back, surprised when her back bumped into the edge of the bar. He brought his hands up, and his fingers slid up her stomach, across the dark fabric, and closed around her breasts. Inhaling sharply, she didn't dare to move. She knew just what his kind was capable of, and she wouldn't be strong enough to stop him if he forced himself on her.

"It won't be long until that righteousness is fucked out of you, little whore," he hissed. His mouth was a breath away from hers.

She didn't bother telling him she wasn't one of the mistresses.

"Perhaps I'll educate you myself." His eyes raked over her, and her skin felt hot and prickly. It was nothing like what she'd felt for the vampire.

Slowly, he lowered his hands, and she breathed a sigh of relief as the pressure on her breasts lifted. Nearby lantern light glinted off the start of sharp fangs.

A vampire, she realized. *He's a vampire—who sells other vampires.*

"If you've got such a soft heart, you can tend to his wounds," the ringleader said as he turned on a heel, gesturing to where the vampire kneeled on the stage. "I won't pay for your blood this time."

It was then she realized the vampire's eyes were fixed on them, full of icy fire.

Two of the ringleader's massive guards flanked her, and she strode wordlessly to the stage. She wondered if they were vampires, too. It would explain how the troupe had traveled across the demon-infested roads and survived.

Patrons lingered around the seats, watching her every movement. She was relieved her legs didn't tremble as she strode atop the stage and reached for where the vampire's chains were locked on to the ring on the floor.

"I'm sorry," she whispered as she released the hook and his chains rattled free.

She wasn't sure what she was apologizing for exactly. The establishment? The auctions? The fact that he was being treated as something far less than human?

Her eyes settled on his back where angry red lines stretched from side to side and across the backs of his arms. There were traces of blood, but the wounds had closed at least. They looked far less angry than the skin beneath the shackles at his wrists and neck. The shackles around his ankles had a layer of fabric between them and his skin.

The vampire didn't respond. Instead, he looked up at her, his gaze sweeping over her face.

Desolation filled in his eyes, and it took her breath away.

If what Jonas said was true, this male had been turned when he was newly into adulthood. While his jawline was sharp and his chest broad and muscled, there was a youthful air she couldn't quite name. He didn't feel like the ancient vampires who'd come through Shadowbank in secret in years past who cloaked themselves in the memories of the ages. Instead, he felt like a peer. One who had seen far too much of the world.

"Please," she said. "Come with me."

Standing, she turned, not bothering to grab the vampire's chains. He wasn't a dog, and she wasn't about to pull him around like the ringleader had. Neither of the guards flanking her reached for the silver chains.

At the sound of rattling chains behind her, she knew the vampire was following.

The crowd parted for them, allowing them to walk by. Every head turned, skating up and down the length of the vampire's body, completely unseeing of his wounds.

Disgust roiled in her stomach, but she kept her face neutral as she strode past them to the back of the room and down a narrow hallway lit by a single lantern before she opened the door to one of the soundproof rooms she'd seen earlier that day. Cells would have been a better description. There were wooden floors, wooden walls, and a wooden ceiling. No furniture, and no windows. She'd wondered what they were for earlier, but now she knew. She also knew this was where Jonas expected her to take him.

She gestured for the vampire to enter, which he did without a word.

Suddenly, a large hand was on her shoulder, shoving her forward and into the room after him. The door closed, locking behind them—with the guards on the other side.

"We'll be back in a few minutes after he's fed," one guard called through the door. "If you're still alive, that is."

Growling, she pushed herself to her feet and brushed off the dirt on her dress before turning to where a lantern hung beside the door. Lighting it, she turned back toward the room, and there was a flash of movement and jingle of metal on metal.

The vampire was before her, fangs out, and standing unnaturally still.

Her heart raced. Even though every instinct within her screamed to run, that she was in danger, she could only look up at the male—her eyes tracing across his sharp jawline to his dark brows to his short black hair that came to his eyes.

His gaze darted down to her neck—to the very spot he'd bitten her before and was now hidden by a scarf. Hunger filled his eyes.

Her heartbeat quickened, and she forced herself to take several deep breaths.

"What's your name?" she asked, breaking the silence between them.

The male laughed humorlessly, and she realized it was the most emotion she'd seen him express.

"Something funny?" she asked, surprised to feel indignation swelling within her.

"You're the only one who's bothered to ask me that since I was turned."

His voice was like amber honey to her ears, but his words felt like shards of glass scraping against her heart.

He'd been treated like this for a while, then.

"When were you... turned?"

She wasn't sure if he'd want to reveal something so personal. But something inside her had her asking. She wanted to know him, to understand him.

To her surprise, he took a step back and then another until there were several feet between them. But his fangs never disappeared.

"A few months ago," he answered, his blue eyes seeming to darken. Then he sighed. "My name is Rowan."

She nodded. "I'm sorry."

His brows drew together, and his eyes narrowed. "Why are you sorry?"

"Did they give you a choice?" she said, daring to voice what she'd guessed since the moment Jonas revealed Rowan would be auctioned.

Rowan sniffed, his chains rattling as he shifted. "No vampire promised for auction goes of their free will." After a moment, he added, "Many of the vampires in Jonas' troupe choose this life. Usually to escape another, but they become vampires willingly. For a price, of course."

When she frowned, not understanding, he said, "Ten years of service in exchange for immortality. That's Jonas' terms. A fair bargain if they survive, I suppose."

"How does one become a vampire?" she asked, her voice sounding small even to her ears.

"Blood," he said. "You have to ingest vampire blood before you die—and drink mortal blood within a day of waking."

Of course, she thought.

Smoothing her dress unnecessarily, she took a breath and crossed the room toward him.

It took all her focus to ignore the electricity surging through her veins at his nearness. Something about him drew her in, and she wanted to be swept up in the storm. It had to be from his bite. There was no way she could be so attracted to a male she didn't know and had hardly spoken to. But her body thrummed as though, for the first time in her life, she was truly alive.

She wanted to feel his lips on her skin again. Perhaps even more than that, she wanted to see the pain vanish from his gaze.

Pulling her hair off her neck and exposing herself to him, she said, "Take what you need."

Chapter Three

ROWAN

Four simple words.

Take what you need.

At the sound of those words on her lips, Rowan's fangs lengthened further.

Sharp tips pressed into his lips and punctured his skin. The pain paled compared to the agony along the skin at his wrists and neck, but the taste of his blood had him thinking of how her blood had filled his mouth not too long ago—and how her body had been so pliant, so willing beneath his. Yet, the most he could do was grip the red fabric of her dress and greedily drink her in.

Now, she stood in a black dress that hugged her thin frame. He could see the outline of ribs above her small chest, and he wondered how she was treated. While she was as beautiful as a scarlet sunrise, she looked worn down and exhausted. It was in the purple smudges beneath her eyes and in the way her eyelids seemed to droop slightly when she blinked. But even with the tiredness laced through her features, she was an undeniable beauty. She reminded him of a wild stallion.

"Leave now," he hissed through his fangs. "I might rip out your throat if you don't."

Despite his words, he didn't step away from her.

A distant part of him knew she had as little choice in being here as he did. Otherwise, she wouldn't have been locked in this room beside him. Clearly, Jonas thought he'd drink this female dry—save himself the trouble of dealing with her himself.

Even from where she stood a mere arm's reach from him, Rowan could feel the heat of her body. Vampires were far colder than humans. It was part of the reason vampires needed blood to survive—for warmth. He longed to bury himself in her neck, sink his fangs into her, and taste her blood once more.

He'd struggled to think of anything else in the hours since he'd held her.

But like Jonas and his father, she would use him. She was only here because she wanted the feel of a vampire bite and all the pleasure it brought with it. The sympathy in her gaze was a falsity. It was all a game to get what she wanted.

But why had she come to the stage when Jonas whipped him?

"Nemera," she said, her dark eyes flickering between his.

Her eyes were the opposite of her hair—dark as tilled earth—while her hair was the color of fiery sunrises.

"What?"

"My name. It's Nemera."

He blinked, surprised he hadn't asked what her name was before. Hadn't the madam also told him her name? His mind had been so fuzzy with the pain from his back and the agony from the shackles that he must have forgotten something so normal as an exchange of names. But what did it matter if he knew the name of yet another mortal who wanted to use him?

"You're not going to hurt me," Nemera said. "Otherwise, you would've done it already. Besides, you need blood to heal."

Her voice held a lot more confidence than he felt.

His eyes darkened. "If I was free of these chains, and they weren't a constant drain on my strength, I wouldn't be able to stop myself from feasting on your blood. All of your blood. Even now, with these limits on my powers... I might not be able to stop."

His mind conjured the image of her body beneath his, her red curls splayed as he leaned down, licking every inch of her skin before sinking his teeth into her and feeling her blood fill his mouth.

Did females even like that sort of thing? He had no idea. She was likely far more experienced in such things than he was.

Wanting her—wanting anything—was foolish. He must stop this train of thought now or else he might dare to hope for more.

As it was, it took everything in him to remain standing where he was, not to close the distance between them and feast on her.

Her gaze settled on his wrists, red brows drawing together. "It's cruel what Jonas does. He shouldn't—"

"Stop," he said, cutting her off. "Whatever you're about to say, just don't. You're going to make it worse."

Mere months ago, his father had sold him to Jonas. His only family hadn't wanted him—hadn't thought him valuable enough to fight for. Ever since then, he'd learned the extent of the ring-leader's cruelty. It was far easier to obey. It was that or face his wrath. But under Jonas' care, he didn't go hungry. It was an improvement, at least, from his life before.

What if I wasn't bound to Jonas?

Some small part of him rebelled, screaming for someone—anyone—to fight for him. Not once in his life had he been free of hardship. He'd either been under his father's thumb or the ring-leader's.

Nemera walked across the room, the heels of her boots clicking faintly on the floors, until she was before him, their bodies were nearly touching.

"Those lashes look like they hurt," she said, her gaze unflinching. Then she held her hair in one hand, pulling it over her left shoulder and leaving the right side of her neck free for him. "You helped me earlier. Let me help you."

He had no idea what had come over him earlier. He'd found himself moving between Jonas and Nemera, the whip wrapping around his arm as he took the slash that had been meant for her.

His chains rattled as he breathed, her stomach pressing into them.

The scent of her filled his nostrils—strawberries and sunshine. Behind it, he detected the scent of her blood and felt himself salivate.

Just a sip, he thought. *To take off the edge.*

Before he could lean in to accept her offer, she spoke again.

"You don't have to, you know. If it makes you uncomfortable, that is." He heard her swallow. "Only take my blood if you need it —or if you want to take it."

A mortal didn't want his bite? Hearing that he had the option whether to feed, that she expected nothing from him, had his cock growing hard.

Quickly, he placed his hands over his crotch, the chains rattling. He cleared his throat, and his cheeks flushed.

How was it that he was turned on by her *not* expecting something from him? That couldn't be normal. He'd had no one to ask about desiring a woman once he'd grown into his manhood, and he'd been too busy finding work to afford food for his father and himself to even think about finding pleasure in another's body. But damn him, he felt *something* for this woman. He wanted to feel her warm skin against his.

She's just playing with my head, he thought. *Everyone always wants something.*

But if she wanted something from him, perhaps he could get something from her in return.

An idea slowly formed in his mind.

Putting some distance between them, he stepped back, keeping his hands over his cock, which bulged uncomfortably in his pants.

"You want me to feed on you?" he said. "Then I want something in return."

Something to make me less valuable to Jonas.

In his short life, he'd learned that he was only worth as much as his body—either the work he could do or (now) what pleasures he could give others as a vampire. This woman was no different.

To his surprise, she frowned and crossed her arms. Her cheeks turned pink, but he didn't think it was from embarrassment.

"You presume much," she said, her tone as sharp as fractured pottery. "I might have only known Jonas for hours, but I already know what kind of man he is. And he doesn't have a right to sell *anyone* like chattel."

Did she honestly expect him to believe she'd do any of this out of the *kindness* of her heart? No one cared about others more than their own hide.

Rowan couldn't help himself. He scoffed, laughing humorlessly. "How noble of you."

Eyes narrowing, she said, "I'm risking my job by helping you. A job that I need to—never mind. Believe what you want."

"You want to help me? Fine." He allowed the anger he'd put a lid on for weeks to seep into his voice, into his very veins. "Let's pretend I believe you. Then I need something from you."

"Oh?" She didn't uncross her arms. Instead, she raised a brow as though she were *humoring* him.

"In exchange for my bite," he said, "I want you to take my virginity."

To his surprise, her mouth hung open for several moments before she snapped it shut.

"You're serious," she said. It wasn't a question. "Why?"

"Perhaps I won't be such a tempting sale if I'm no longer a virgin."

Maybe Jonas will hire me as one of his grunts, he thought. *If he doesn't try to sell me off at a steep discount once he learns of this.*

He knew he shouldn't fight his fate. He knew that the moment Jonas found out, things were going to become much, much worse for him. But could he willingly become someone's sex slave without at least trying for his freedom? Was he not allowed to wish for a different life for himself?

Still, would someone using his body to satisfy their sexual

needs be so bad? He wouldn't go hungry if he was sold. Whoever took his chains wouldn't want him to go too long without feeding so that they could safely indulge in his bite. He might not even be required to do manual labor for whoever bought him—assuming they'd want to keep it a secret that they'd purchased a vampire. Could such a life be so bad? But even the idea of not having to face severe hunger every single day or work until his back broke wasn't enough to dampen his desire to not be auctioned off.

What was it like to be free? He had no notion. Certainly, it had to be better than this.

Nemera's eyes shifted between his, searching—though for what, he didn't know. Eventually, she dropped her arms and sighed.

"If that's what you want," she said. "But you don't have to bite me. I offered before because I thought you needed it."

Her gaze dropped to his wrists where his skin was raw and red and felt like a deep sun poisoning in the way it burned and blistered. She wasn't wrong. Blood would ease some of the pain. But it would only come back with these handcuffs. The relief would be short-lived at best.

"Fine," he said, swallowing thickly as his heart raced—thankful that she couldn't hear his quickening heartbeat with her human ears.

The idea of holding her naked body had desire hazing his thoughts, making it hard to think straight.

Another part of him wondered what it would be like to no longer glow under the light of the moon. He'd felt like a torch in the darkness on their travels, the blanket barely subduing the light from his skin. The only perk had been that the demons had avoided him and his cage when they'd been attacked on the road.

The sound of Nemera's voice pulled him from his thoughts.

"How old are you?"

He started, the question surprising him. "Twenty-four."

"Me, too." For a moment, she wrapped a few of her curls

around a finger before quickly dropping it. "I don't know if it matters to you, but I was married."

He blinked. "Why would I care about that?"

Did she think he would find her less attractive because she'd once been married?

She shrugged, seeming uncertain for the first time since he'd met her. "If I'm to be your first time... I thought you had a right to know. That I'm not a virgin."

He nodded. After a moment, he said, "I don't mind. As long as you don't mind... guiding me."

Now, it was his turn to blush. Blood rushed to his cheeks, and he forced himself to keep his eyes on this fiery woman who had agreed to help him.

It was best she understood the depth of his inexperience.

One corner of her lips quirked. "Don't worry about that." Then she turned around and stared at the door. "What we need to worry about is how we're going to get you out of here. I'm not about to fuck you on the floor and have one of Jonas' meathead guards come in while we're in the middle of things. How terribly unromantic for your first time."

He frowned.

Was she joking? It didn't matter whether his first time sleeping with a woman was romantic. He just needed it *done* so that these corrupt mortals set on buying him at the auction saw him as *less than*. That, or so Jonas found him a better asset as a guard than something to be sold off.

Suddenly, there was the sound of a key turning in a lock, and the door opened to reveal one of Jonas' vampire guards.

"Time's up," he said, grabbing Nemera's wrist and pulling her from the room.

She glanced over a shoulder, her eyes wide. Was that concern he saw?

But then the door closed, snuffing out the light from the hallway and his view of the dark eyes that pulled him in like a moth to a flame.

HOURS LATER, Rowan had settled himself on the floor, fingering the emerald of his necklace as he stared at the empty wall across from him. The sounds on the other side of the door had long since quieted, and the oil in the lantern was running low.

He must have dozed off because the next he knew, he heard jingle of keys before the door to his cell opened.

The first thing he saw was the light of a single candle before a cloaked figure strode into the room. The figure pushed back the hood of the cloak, revealing a full head of red curls.

"You came back."

The words came out of him before he could stop them. He hadn't thought she'd actually return, but when she closed the door behind her, he felt himself releasing a breath he hadn't realized he'd been holding.

"I told you I would," she said. "The guards are passed out. Drunk. We should have a few hours." She kneeled beside him with what looked like two long needles in one hand. Lockpicks, he realized. She placed the candle on the ground with the other hand, the flame flickering. Then she reached for his cuffs.

To his utter stupidity, he pulled his hands away from her. "Don't."

"Why?"

"I don't know if I'll be able to control myself if you do."

Slowly, she licked her lips. The sight of her pink tongue had something inside of him swirling with desire.

"We'll need to risk taking them off," she said, her eyes fixed on the cuffs. "Ignoring the fact that they probably hurt like hell, they're loud. If we leave them on, we might be discovered while sneaking around the building."

She was right. He knew she was right. But he was far too inexperienced in so many things. And in this, her life would be the consequence if he failed to control himself. Did she regard her life with such little value to risk it in this way?

Slowly, he offered his wrists to her. "Do it, then."

As she worked the lockpicks, she said, "Why didn't you ask me to help you escape?"

Damn, this woman was perceptive.

"Where would I run?" he said, biting back the pain as the cuffs pressed into his raw skin. "I'm a vampire, remember? I can't stay here. Not openly. I'd be kicked out of the village. And I have no money for passage to where my kind can co-exist beside humans."

"You want to work for Jonas," she said as one of his cuffs clicked open. It wasn't a question.

"Maybe."

If he was less valuable—not enough to sell—then maybe the ringleader would let him work for the troupe for the next ten years. Maybe he wouldn't be dressed in silver for the rest of his days.

A few minutes later, Nemera had unlocked the cuffs around his wrists and ankles and the collar around his neck. As she unlocked each one, he started breathing from his mouth—afraid the smell of her blood would make him lose control.

A deep relief settled on his shoulders as the cuffs dropped to the ground with a soft thud. He took several gasping breaths through his mouth, palms on the floor. The pain that he'd been experiencing since he'd been turned—and immediately put into chains—was gone. It no longer felt like his flesh was on fire, burning from the touch of the metal.

"Thank you," he said and meant it.

"No one should be treated like you have." She stood, grabbing the candle, and extending a hand to him. "Follow me."

Chapter Four

NEMERA

When Nemera allowed herself to fantasize about sneaking a man up to her room, it had been nothing like this—with a virgin vampire who wanted her to take his virginity.

Rowan followed closely behind her, and she hurried him down the back hallways and up into the staff's quarters. They had been luckier than the lord of the underworld himself that Jonas' guards had drunk themselves into a stupor and were fast asleep on either side of the door they'd been locked behind.

They passed a window with glass panes that let in the moon's light. As they did, she noticed that her shadow darkened as though a sudden light appeared behind her. Frowning, she turned around, and her breath escaped her.

Rowan glowed as though he were the moon itself. A shimmering opaque light emitted from every inch of his skin, as pale as his fair skin. It reminded her of the reflection of starlight off still water—bright and dark and beautiful all at once.

Realizing she'd been gaping, she shut her mouth.

"Virgin," the vampire said, eyes rolling. "I look forward to not being a personal torch."

Not knowing what to say, she nodded.

What he wanted to do with his body was his choice, but some small part of her felt sad at the idea of taking this from him.

What the fuck am I doing? This is only going to end badly.

This—her being here, *helping* him—was a terrible idea. Jonas would find out tomorrow when he saw Rowan that he wasn't a virgin anymore. And even if Rowan didn't reveal it was her who'd helped him, the ringleader would guess. It was obvious after she'd come to the stage tonight and stopped him from whipping Rowan.

Would she lose her job? Would Trista let Jonas hurt her, use her body as compensation?

Even with the threat of the unknown repercussions, she didn't have the heart to stop. Rowan reminded her of what she'd been when she'd been living in the streets—alone and desperate for help. She couldn't let him fend for himself. Damn her bleeding heart, but she had to help him.

When they arrived at her room, the hallway was utterly silent and empty of her other colleagues. Many would be asleep or bedding clients. Others would still be working in the common room. Patrons wouldn't leave for a few more hours, which meant they had a few more hours of sounds to drown out anything they might be doing.

Inserting a key into the lock, she opened the door to her room and ushered Rowan inside before following and locking it shut behind them. With a sigh of relief, she turned on a lantern, which illuminated the small space in a warm, yellow light.

Like most who worked and boarded at the House of Obscurities, her room was barely big enough for a bed, a side table, and a single set of drawers. The bed could fit two people if they liked to cuddle in the night. Shared washrooms were down the hall. But she had a small hearth at the end of her bed.

It was a humble space, she knew, and she wondered just what Rowan thought of where he'd lose his virginity. She wished there was more she could do to make his first time special. It was what she would have wanted for herself. As it was, she could barely afford this room, let alone one of the suites. But she could make sure that everything they did was consenting—something Rowan wanted.

To her surprise, he stood stiffly at the corner of the bed near the door, appearing as though he planned to bolt for the hallway.

She bit her lip.

She knew they should hurry. Even though the guards were fast asleep, there was no telling when they'd wake up or when Jonas would return to check on them. It could be in minutes or tomorrow morning. But she found she didn't have the heart to hurry this for Rowan.

Instead, she gestured to the nearby window that had the curtains drawn back. "Would you like me to close it?"

He shook his head. "I want to see when it's finally gone."

She nodded and then waved a hand toward the bed and said, "Please. Sit."

"I..." Rowan began but stopped. His eyes skated across the room before flickering between his feet. His bare chest rose and fell in quickening breaths.

He's nervous, she realized. *Really nervous.*

He walked over to the bed and lowered himself onto it.

She took a step toward him and then another until they were within arm's reach.

"I'll only do what you want," she said. "Say the word, and this stops. Okay?"

He seemed to hold his breath for a moment before exhaling and nodding.

"What... What do I do?" he asked, the hardness that had been in his voice and eyes receding.

She thought of how he'd covered himself earlier when she offered her neck to him. Perhaps the thought of feeding on her turned him on. But he'd also been clearly upset by the idea of feeding on her, and she couldn't blame him—not when he was about to be sold for his bite. She wouldn't offer herself to him again, not until he asked first.

Unbidden, she recalled when he'd fed off her on the stage and how he'd held on to her so gently, feeling as though he'd never let go.

Closing the distance between them, she placed herself between his legs where he sat on the bed and said, "Touch me."

She was careful not to touch him, to let him set the pace. If he'd never had a sexual partner before, he was likely eager to get to know the female body—to explore just what it was the bards sang so much about.

His eyes soaked in the sight of her in the black dress, following along the curves of her chest, down to her waist and hips, and back until he met her eyes. It felt nothing like the patrons, whose oily gazes skated over her body, making her feel dirty. Instead, her heartbeat quickened, and she found herself longing to feel his touch.

Ever so slowly, he raised his hands until they fell on the small of her waist.

His fingers skirted a few inches down her hips, squeezing gently. He avoided touching her ass as though out of politeness. Moving down over her legs, he lingered on her thighs. To her surprise, his fingers traced the line where her dress met the bare skin of her legs. He didn't reach beneath her dress, didn't move it up. Instead, he moved a single finger along where the fabric met her thigh in a circle, starting at one leg and then doing the same to the next. Her breath hitched, but she didn't move, allowing him to explore her body.

"Do you like men or women?" she asked, her voice sounding strangely breathy.

She'd slept with her husband more times than she liked to think about. While she had enough experience in penetration, there had been little touching before the act or after. This attention from Rowan was... addicting if she was being honest. It felt like he was trying to memorize every curve and valley of her body.

"Women," he said, his eyes still fixed on her. "I've never experienced attraction to other men. Though I suppose it's possible. What about you?"

Her breaths quickened as his exploration moved up her body to her sides, and his thumbs moved in soft strokes beneath her breasts. She was certain he could hear just what her body thought of his administrations with his sharp vampire senses.

"Men," she managed, longing to grab his wrists and place his hands on her breasts. But she kept them at her sides.

Nodding, he glanced up at her, his thumbs pausing their tantalizing movements beneath her breasts. "What was your first time like?"

"My husband was drunk and forced himself on me after our private nuptials," she said simply. "It was nothing special."

"Was every time like that?"

Her mouth suddenly went dry, and she licked her lips. Damn him. Why was he asking? Was she that transparent? Did he see her like an injured bird he had to handle with care? She didn't want his pity. But she also didn't want to lie.

"Often," she said, choosing to stick strictly to the facts of her past. "My parents arranged the marriage when they saw I'd taken a liking to him. There wasn't really a courting period. We just got married, and I knew immediately it was a mistake. But I was stuck."

His hands dropped to her waist as his brows drew together. "What happened to him?"

"Gone," she said simply.

He nodded. "Good."

"I might be rid of him, but he took everything," she said. "He gambled away all our savings and our home. My parents disowned me when the marriage ended. I lost everything. It's why I'm here —at the House of Obscurities. It was work or continue to live in the streets."

Rowan's eyes flicked between hers, and she thought she saw genuine sadness there. "Fuck him. I'm sorry for what happened to you. You didn't deserve any of it."

One hand lingered on her waist, but he raised the other and ran it through his hair. It made his black hair stick up in sections, and she found it strangely charming.

She allowed a finger to skirt down his arm, marveling at his glowing skin. The moonlight streamed in from the window behind him.

Then he broke the silence. "What do you like, Nemera?"

She paused.

Even her husband had never asked that before.

Should she tell Rowan the truth? She knew what it would sound like given the circumstances that brought him here. But she decided she owed him honesty.

"Squeeze my breasts, and kiss my neck," she said, her heart beating even faster. "You don't have to feed on me if you don't want to. Just... kiss me."

Slowly, the vampire stood to his feet, and she realized then he was much taller than her—her head coming to his chin. She also suddenly remembered that he wasn't wearing a shirt. When he stood, her eyes fell on his bare chest. His nipples were hard, and even in the darkened room, she could see the outlines of his abs in the lantern light. His wasn't a body of someone who sat idle all day. The muscles rippling along his arms, chest, and stomach suggested someone who'd worked long hours in a job that required manual labor. She wondered just what his life had been like before Jonas had taken him.

His hands skirted up until they hovered over her breasts, but then he paused.

Frowning, she looked up at him, and his eyes settled on her lips.

"I'll try to be gentle, but I... I don't know what I'm capable of," he said.

"I'm not made of glass," she said. "I *want* you to touch me."

Then he closed the distance between their bodies, his hands encircling her breasts. His fingers were long and lean, covering her entire breasts. When he squeezed, her eyes fluttered closed, and her head tilted back. No one had touched her in this way, and she didn't realize until that moment how much she'd been craving the touch of a lover—a true lover. Not someone who would just take from her body and leave her feeling vulnerable and unsatisfied.

Then she felt him lean forward before the satin softness of his lips was against her neck.

She gasped.

"Rowan," she whispered into the darkness, surprised to find his name on her tongue but liking it all the same.

He made a sound against her skin, and she wasn't sure if it was a moan or something else. Whatever it was, she liked it.

His lips moved from the sensitive skin where her neck met her collarbone up to the shell of her ear. It was her weakness—the touch of a lover on her neck—and she melted into him. One of his arms wrapped around her lower back, and the other never stopped touching her chest. The touch was so good, too good, that she thought she'd scream. She wanted more of him. She *needed* more of him, needed to touch him.

Unable to hold herself back any longer, she wrapped her arms around his back. Part of her must have expected to feel soft skin or perhaps coarse hair like her husband's back. Instead, her fingers fell on the hard ridges of what could only be scars on his back, as though he'd been whipped many times before tonight.

A hand caught her wrist, and her eyes fluttered open.

"Don't," he hissed.

She nodded, and he released her. She could respect that certain parts of him were off-limits. Perhaps there were emotional scars as well that he wasn't ready to address yet, and she could understand that.

Slowly, she moved her hands to his chest, running her fingers along his collarbone before playing with his nipples.

He moaned then.

"Do that again," he said, and the sheer vulnerability in his voice surprised her. "Please."

She swirled her fingers around his nipples, feeling satisfaction as they pebbled beneath her touch.

"Like this?"

His mouth opened and closed as though he struggled to find the words.

"I want your mouth on them, I think."

She nodded and leaned down, not needing further encouragement.

A growing part of her longed to feel his pleasure beneath her touch. She wanted to be the reason he came undone. Never had she felt anything like it—the desire to please another person. Before, she had simply been the recipient, the tool for a man's pleasure. There hadn't been the option for anything more, and she hadn't dared to ask. Part of her hadn't wanted to for fear of a repercussion. The idea of touching her husband made her stomach turn and the flesh between her legs go dry.

But as she leaned down, pressing her palms against Rowan's cold chest and running her tongue around his nipples, desire shot down to her core. She stifled a moan at the sound of a gasp from Rowan from where he stood above her. Slowly, she did the same to his other nipple. Then she put the bud into her mouth and *sucked*.

He moaned, the sound breathy and raw.

"Just like that," he whispered as his hands tangled in her curls.

She swirled her tongue around his nipple while sucking it, feeling her nails scrape against his chest without her willing it to. It was as though she couldn't get close enough to him. She needed to feel him everywhere, to feel him deep inside of her.

What was happening?

She had to slow down. This was his first time, and she wanted to do right by him.

Moving to his other nipple, she did likewise and earned another soft moan.

Just what sounds would he make if she went down on him?

Rising, she reached for his pants, unlatching his belt. "I want you to lie down on the bed."

Nodding, he watched as she unfastened his trousers and pulled them down. She removed his boots and the rest of his clothes until he was completely naked before her.

He was exquisite.

Like his chest and stomach, there wasn't an ounce of fat on him. His legs were long and lean, and the lantern light glowed against his fair skin. She could kiss every inch of those legs, which were covered in a faint layer of hair that was as dark as the hair on his head and never get enough of him. Shifting her eyes back up to his cock, she bit her lower lip. His cock was long, and the tip glistened with a bead of moisture.

He wanted her.

That thought made something inside of her ignite, and butterflies fluttered in her stomach even as the flesh between her legs grew wet. She wanted to straddle this male and sink onto his perfect cock. She wanted to wrap her hand around his balls and feel them shift between her fingers.

Soon, she thought. And then she looked up at him.

His eyes raked over her before meeting his gaze, pleading and uncertain. In that moment, she knew he was going to be an eager lover.

Raising her hands, she gently pressed his shoulders, indicating for him to lie down. He did without a word, shifting to the center of the bed, his eyes never leaving hers.

"I'm going to kiss you," she said. "On your stomach, hips, and your cock."

When his eyes skirted to her lips, she realized then that they had yet to actually kiss. Somehow, that felt even more intimate than what she was about to do.

He nodded, and she joined him on the bed, pressing his legs wider before placing herself between them. Leaning forward, she put her arms on either side of his chest and pressed a kiss to his left nipple, swirling her tongue around it again. There was an intake of breath as she kissed down his chest, sucking and nipping.

For a moment, she lingered at the place where his legs met his hips, running her tongue along it. She was rewarded with his cock twitching and his whole body stretching out.

He fisted the sheets and said, "Wait."

ROWAN FELT FIT TO BURST.

Nemera's touch alone had him about to unravel, and she hadn't even touched his cock.

He knew that if she wrapped those luscious pink lips around his cock, he would unleash in her in mere moments. And to lose his virginity and this incessant glow, he'd need to have fucked a woman... fucked Nemera in those sweet folds of hers.

The sweet folds he had yet to touch.

"I won't last long if you do that," he said from where he lay on his back, looking down at her between his legs. The sight of her there did something inside of him that he didn't dare name.

She nodded as though she understood.

Frowning, he wondered, not for the first time, why she was so patient with him. She was here to use him for his bite. So, why be so kind to him?

He leaned up in the bed, and she did likewise so that she kneeled across from him.

"I can bite you now, if you'd like," he said. "A deal's a deal. Then we can..."

She raised her brows. "Have sex, you mean?" She smiled, cocking her head to the side. "You're not what I expected." Then she shook her head. "I told you. You don't have to bite me unless you need to."

Swallowing, he said, "Why are you helping me?"

"No one deserves to be treated the way Jonas has treated you. If this is going to help, I'd like to give this to you."

There seemed to be something else she wasn't saying, but he nodded.

She doesn't want to use me, some part of him thought, unable to wrap his mind fully around that. It felt too good to be real. Certainly, it couldn't be.

It didn't matter. They'd fuck, and then they'd go their separate ways. It was only sex.

But why did it feel like so much more?

Rising on her knees, she pulled her dress over her head. As it slid up her thin body, revealing her pale skin inch by inch, his eyes fixed on the path the dress took until she removed it and tossed it on the floor. Then she was naked before him.

While she was thin, perhaps too much so, her beauty cascaded into the room around them as though she glowed from within. As though she were the virgin vampire with skin as bright as the moon. Some distant part of him yearned to take care of her, to cook her dinner, and bring her wildflowers to loop into her wilder curls.

Tearing his mind from thoughts of her smile and lazy summer afternoons, he allowed lust to fill him at the sight of her. Her legs were long and pale like porcelain, and her stomach looked like it had been sculpted by the gods themselves. If such creatures existed. The lantern light caught the dips in her hips leading to her...

He swallowed.

Short red hair, as bright as the hair on her head, filled his gaze.

He wanted to bury his face in her. But the knowledge that he had no idea what the hell he was doing had him remaining where he was.

She pressed a hand to his chest, and he allowed her to push him back onto the bed until he lay on his back once more. Then she moved until her legs were on either side of his hips and her pussy hovered in the air just above his erect cock.

Fuck. He wanted her. He never wanted anything so much in his life.

His skin glowed brightly, reminding him of everything he was —all he was being used for. And he hated it. He'd wanted none of this, and he certainly never thought of his virginity as anything special. If losing his supposed innocence meant he had a chance at a better life, then he wanted nothing more than to be rid of it.

But if he was being honest with himself, he had another reason he wanted to lose his virginity. One he hadn't expected to want so quickly—and so deeply. He wanted to lose himself in this woman.

Reaching up, he fingered the emerald pendant of his necklace.

"Tell me to stop if you need to," Nemera said, her eyes flickering between his.

To his surprise, something like a growl escaped his lips, and he grabbed her hips in either hand, marveling at the softness of her skin. Then brought her down onto him—sheathing himself inside of her.

It felt so good that he moaned instantly, his head tilting back.

When he blinked his eyes open, she was watching him, lust filling her gaze. Then something else filled her gaze. It was both wonder and sadness, he thought, as the glow of his skin faded from its bright iridescence until it resembled any other vampire.

He'd done it. It was gone.

But he was far from through with this woman.

As though letting go of hesitation, of any restraint, she began riding him in earnest.

She was hot and wet all around him. There was a delicious wet slap every time she came down on him.

She was wet. For him.

The idea that someone wanted him had something inside of him stirring. He'd always been the poor bastard of a drunkard of a father—not worth enough to even keep around. But this woman made him feel like he was more than an inconvenience. Like he was someone worth wanting.

She never stopped moving, placing her hands on his chest as

she did. Her nails sunk into him as she moved her hips in a circular motion even as she moved up and down on his cock.

"Fuck," he hissed, his fingers squeezing her hips as though willing her to go faster.

She was decadent. She was the morning star, engulfing him in light. She was warmth itself. The warmth of her cunt felt downright sinful against him.

Sex with her was unlike anything he'd ever imagined, far better than any release he'd gotten from his hands. It was ecstasy.

Letting go fully into this moment, this time with her, he grabbed her hips and began fucking her from where he lay. She fell forward, catching herself on her hands, which pressed into the bed on either side of him. But she allowed him to lead.

Leaning up, he placed a kiss on her neck before licking the soft skin behind her ear. She made a sound like a whimper as he thrust up into her, never stopping.

He didn't know what the hell he was doing. All he knew was that he wanted her—wanted to kiss every inch of her skin and claim her for this moment. For this night. Because that was all they had. All they could ever have.

Pleasure thrummed inside his chest and bolted down to his cock. He wouldn't last much longer. She was going to be his undoing.

"Do you want me to come inside of you?" he managed past the haze of lust that threatened to pull him under. "I... I don't know if I can time it and pull out before."

He was too new to this, his body too eager.

It wasn't possible for vampires to make humans pregnant. But perhaps it was something she wouldn't be comfortable with.

"Come in my mouth," she said, pulling herself off him.

He let go of her hips as she settled herself between his legs once more.

As he looked down, he noticed her slickness all over his cock. The evidence of her desire for him. It made the fire burning inside of him intensify even more.

Without a moment's hesitation, she leaned down, grabbing the base of his cock in one hand. Then her mouth was around him. Her lips were as soft as he thought they'd be. She was warm and wet, and it felt both similar and entirely different from her pussy. He knew he wouldn't be able to get enough of either.

She moved up and down his shaft, her hand's movements timed with her mouth. Slowly, his hips moved of their own volition, fucking her mouth.

"I... I'm going to come," he managed, his voice cracking.

Then he was coming undone. He cried out as pleasure cascaded over him. He burst inside her mouth, feeling his seed spill into her. She drank him down, sucking and licking his shaft.

When he was spent, she rose to her knees and wiped her lower lip with her thumb, her eyes never leaving his.

Grabbing the shreds of his courage, he said, "Now, it's my turn. Lie back."

Chapter Five

NEMERA

For a moment, Nemera forgot how to speak.

"You don't have to do that," she said. "Tonight was for you."

To her surprise, Rowan frowned as if those were the most preposterous words ever spoken by humankind. Then he said, "Would you deny me on my first night? Having sex wouldn't be complete without you getting your pleasure as well."

The way he spoke, it was so matter of fact. As though men didn't use women's bodies all the time for their pleasure without ever reciprocating—as if that wasn't the case most nights for the mistresses who worked in the House.

Likely sensing the direction of her thoughts, he said, "Did I say something wrong?"

She shook her head. "No one has thought about my pleasure in this way before."

The lines between his brows deepened. "Your ex-husband never wanted to give you release?"

Her throat became tight, and she shook her head. "He was more of a get-in-and-get-out kind of man after he got what he wanted."

"I know as much about sex as I do about being a vampire," he began. "But even I know his actions are selfish and despicable. I'm sorry."

Something inside her chest squeezed. "Why are you apologizing?"

"It seems we were both dealt a shit hand in this life."

She shifted where she kneeled before him, suddenly uncertain what to do with her hands. "How did you end up here? With Jonas, I mean."

"My father sold me," he said, his eyes falling to his hands as he opened and closed them.

His words were like the blunt edge of a blade and spoken without a hint of emotion. Hesitating, she wasn't sure whether to speak or allow him the silence to find his words—should he want to share anything else.

Eventually, she said, "I shouldn't have asked. You don't have to share anything you don't want to."

Eyes still fixed on his open palms, he said, "I want at least one person to know me." He took a deep breath. "I'm the bastard son of the town's drunk. My birth mother dropped me off at his door the day I was born. I never knew her."

Her throat tightened, but she didn't dare to speak or move.

"I worked any job I could since I was a child," he continued. "Before my father sold me, I worked as a laborer on local farms and in some failing mines. I made enough for us to get by. One night, men came by, and my father was given a single day to pay off his gambling debts. Jonas and his troupe were traveling through the town. My father offered me to him in exchange for what he owed. When my father revealed I was untouched—a virgin—Jonas accepted. I didn't fight it. I let Jonas shove his blood down my throat and snap my neck. When I woke up, I was already in silver chains, and he forced me to drink human blood. Then I was a vampire—and a glowing one at that."

Disgust filled her. How could anyone be this cruel—to turn someone into a vampire against their will? For a father to sell his own son? It was beyond anything she could fathom. Rowan had never asked for this life. Beyond the emotional impact of all of this, had becoming a vampire been painful? He'd been through so much.

Unbidden, she reached out and clasped his hand, holding it between both of hers.

"What happened to you was terrible," she said, tears streaming down her cheeks. "You did nothing wrong. You didn't deserve any of this."

His eyes found hers then, and he blinked as though trying to wrap his mind around her words.

She took a deep breath before adding, "I'm glad I met you, Rowan."

A faint smile crept over his normally serious features, and she smiled in return. She realized then it was the first time she'd seen him smile.

As though realizing what he was doing, the smile disappeared, and he cleared his throat.

She ran her thumb over the top of his hand. "Do that again."

"Do what?"

"Smile," she said.

Reaching out, he placed his other hand over hers where she still held on to him. "Perhaps I can make *you* smile... or moan. Either is fine with me."

Then he offered the most cheeky grin to her, and she laughed.

"I like the sound of your laugh," he said.

Something swirled in her chest, and she fumbled for words. Eventually, she settled on, "Thank you."

Then he was shifting so that he knelt before her and gently guided her to where he was just lying. "You'll have to direct me. I want to know what you like."

Trying to shake off the darkness of their pasts, she allowed herself to be in this moment with him. She lay down, and he spread her legs, his eyes feasting on her like she was the most beautiful thing he'd ever seen.

A sudden wave of self-consciousness swept over her. For a

moment, words were beyond her reach. But as she'd decided before, she owed him honesty if nothing else. So, she dared to say the words she'd never shared with anyone before.

"I don't know if I can come," she said, her voice soft. Even she could hear the vulnerability in it. "I've never... It's never happened for me before."

"You've never touched yourself?" he asked, seeming surprised.

She shook her head. Such things were frowned upon in the culture she grew up in. So, she never did. Not even in the time she'd been with her husband and was left wanting, her body taut with dissatisfaction.

"I look forward to learning your body together, then," he said as he settled himself between her legs. "In whatever time we have left."

And who knew how much time that was? It could be anything from minutes to hours, depending on when Rowan's absence was discovered.

Brows furrowing, she said the only words she could think of. "How are you real?"

Another smile lit his face before he leaned down and flicked a tentative tongue over her entrance. "Does this feel real?"

She reached a hand behind her, fisting the pillow.

"Yes."

Again, he ran his tongue over her sensitive folds. This time, he continued until she felt him flick his tongue against her clit.

"There," she gasped. "Do that again there."

Glancing down, she saw he was looking up at her as though assessing her reaction. Then he turned his eyes back to her clit, running his tongue over it in a languid motion. At first, he moved in slow circles, shifting her folds as he explored every hill and valley of her. The way his movements were entirely unhurried, it had her body growing slack and pliant. She realized then what felt so different. He wasn't in a hurry for her to climax—eager to finish her and get back to his pleasure.

It was as though he was enjoying her, that it wasn't about the destination. As though he truly cared.

But that wasn't possible. They were strangers. He couldn't want more for her than her husband had. He only wanted this night, and that's all she could want, too.

Even as the thoughts flashed through her mind, he buried himself between her legs with such enthusiasm that she felt something in her core tingle. A delicious pressure built in her lower stomach unlike anything she'd experienced before. The way he touched her, licked her, buried himself inside of her... It was as though he needed to feel her as much as he needed his next breath.

Still fisting a pillow in one hand, her other hand strayed down until it tangled in his black hair.

He stiffened for a second, slowing his pace as she moved herself against him. Then he shifted the movements of his tongue until he moved up and down over her clit.

Her back bowed, and she gasped. "Don't stop."

He didn't reply. Instead, his tongue continued its movements in long, steady strokes, and the pressure in her core grew even tighter—so tight that she didn't know how much longer she could take it. She began moving her hips against him in earnest, letting her body do as it willed, moving on instinct.

There was something that felt so right about this male. Between her legs. It felt like this was the very thing she had been longing for. She didn't dare examine those feelings further.

The pleasure was torturous. But it wasn't enough. She wanted more.

She wanted to be filled by him.

"I want you," she rasped. "I need to be filled again."

Glancing up, brows furrowed, he said, "I'm not ready yet, I don't think. But... perhaps there's something else I can do."

Shifting, he brought his arm up so that his fingers stroked over her slick folds. He moved them over where his tongue had just been before lowering his hand until...

Oh.

Wow.

His finger was inside of her.

He plunged into her like he had with his cock before, in and out and back. Then he lowered his face over her again, his tongue returning to the up-and-down motion he'd been doing before on her clit.

"Rowan," she gasped. A moan escaped her lips, and she covered her mouth, afraid of making too much noise in case anyone was in the hallway—or in search of them.

But even the thought of Jonas and the auction couldn't reach her. Not here. Not with this male.

Instead, she moved against his face, and he never stopped fucking her with his finger and his tongue.

Too soon, the pressure in her core exploded, and pleasure washed over her. It felt like her every sense was on fire, stars bursting inside her mind. She didn't move her hand from her mouth as she cried out, her body twitching and trembling. It was unlike anything she'd experienced. *He* was unlike anything she'd experienced.

When her orgasm subsided, she opened her eyes, not recalling having closed them.

Looking down, she watched as Rowan pulled his finger from inside her before putting it in his mouth and *sucking*.

Fuck.

"I might be ready again soon," he said, never breaking eye contact with her.

The corner of her lips lifted. "Let's see where the night takes us."

Damn her, but she didn't want this night to end.

He raised himself to a seated position, and she did likewise. To her surprise, he reached back to the necklace with the emerald pendant and leather strap he'd been wearing since the first time she'd seen him. Then he offered it to her, palm up. "I'd like for you to have this."

Brows furrowing, she said, "I don't need payment, Rowan. I—"

He shook his head. "It's not that. In my father's culture, men make a necklace when they come of age, and they wear these necklaces until the first time they lie with a woman—or their chosen partner." With a shrug, he gestured to the pendant in his palm. "You're my first."

She opened and closed her mouth. After a moment, she nodded, and he leaned forward, holding each end of the leather cord in either hand. "May I?"

When she said yes, he reached around and tied it behind her neck. She tried to steady her racing heart at his nearness. His chest was at eye level, and he was still entirely and utterly naked.

Fuck, but she wanted to go again.

Once finished, he leaned back and looked down to where the emerald had settled between her breasts. He smiled, stretched a hand out, and traced a single finger over it before lowering his arm and leaning back.

"Thank you," he said. "For accepting it and for... everything."

Heat crept into her cheeks, and she cleared her throat. "You have nothing to thank me for."

Uncertainty filled his gaze before he said, "How was it?"

"Exquisite," she said without hesitation. "You were amazing."

And I want you again.

Suddenly, his eyes darkened and grew distant. "I guess I'll be the ideal sex slave, then."

"No," she said, shaking her head, a strange fear filling her chest. Then words were tumbling out of her lips—words she hadn't dared voice until that moment. "Don't go back. Get out of here before Jonas realizes you're gone."

"I have nowhere to go."

"Leave Shadowbank," she said. "Find somewhere you can be happy."

And safe.

The hardness returned to his gaze. "I don't have money for passage."

She thought of the moments after she'd learned her husband had abandoned her, and she was completely destitute—without a home or way to financially support herself. At that moment, she swore she'd never let a man control her money, and she'd never be vulnerable like that ever again. In the years she'd been working at the House of Obscurities, she'd saved toward starting her life over and maybe having a home of her own again one day. She wasn't sure what that new life looked like yet, but she knew she needed money to make the choice. And she'd worked hard every day since.

Her gaze lingered on the male before her with hair as dark as night and skin paler than the face of the moon. His jawline was sharp, his face clean-shaven. And he had large lips that she still longed to kiss. There was an innocence that lingered about him, a vulnerability he didn't want anyone to see. He'd been forced to face this cruel world alone.

Don't do it, she thought. *Don't you dare give everything up for a man* again.

But even as she had the thought, she opened her mouth to speak.

"Don't worry about payment," she said. "I'll help you."

Damn her for a fool, but she would help this male if he let her.

And then he's going to leave me trapped in this life.

She'd be working at the House of Obscurities for the rest of her life—that was *if* she didn't lose her job the moment Jonas and Trista found out what she'd done. Maybe she'd be living on the streets again.

But she didn't share that aloud. It was more important for him to get away from Jonas than it was for her to start a new life. At least, she wasn't being sold to be used on the whims of strangers.

At least, she wouldn't be auctioned.

She'd survived on the streets of Shadowbank before, and she'd do so again if she must.

If they were going to get him to safety, they had to leave, and soon. That was—if Jonas hadn't already realized they were gone and hunted for them.

She took a breath and spoke the damning words, the words that would trap her in this life.

"Do you want my help?"

Chapter Six

ROWAN

Several hours later, the cool dawn air dusted Rowan's shoulders as he stood before the docks of Shadowbank, a village at the cusp of survival—holding its breath until the next demon attack.

At this early hour, there weren't many people out. Only the sailors who prepared ships for departure moved about the docks, carrying goods onto the ships.

Three ships were docked.

Cloaked in shadows, he and Nemera stood in a nearby alley, eyeing the surroundings for Jonas and his vampire guards.

Rowan should feel fear at the potential of creatures of the deep attacking the vessel. He should feel fear at the potential of Jonas catching up with him. Yet, he felt nothing.

Nothing but numbness.

He'd been the equivalent of an indentured servant to his father. Without ever being asked what he wanted, he'd taken on the role of caregiver. Then his father had sold him to the ring-leader, and he'd been forced to become a vampire against his will.

Now, this woman was giving him a choice. Perhaps the first choice he'd been given in his life. He should feel grateful to her.

Instead, the idea of leaving in a matter of minutes and never seeing her again had something inside of his chest twisting.

Stretching out a hand, Nemera passed him a large coin purse, and he reluctantly accepted it. He blinked, surprised by the weight. There had to be a hundred coins or more in here. It was far more than what Jonas had paid her for her blood. Was this a year's wages? More?

"This should get you off the continent," she said, eyes lingering for a moment too long on the purse. "If these ships aren't going more than a few villages over or to the capital, you should be able to afford passage from one ship there off the continent. Jonas wouldn't be able to find you then."

The weight of the coin purse settled into his sweating palm, but he didn't move to tuck it into his cloak—yet another thing this woman had given to him. It was a nondescript cloak that she'd said belonged to one of her colleagues. She'd said she'd reimburse him for it, but Rowan didn't like the idea of being so indebted to anyone.

She gestured toward the three ships that were docked, two of which had crewmembers moving around even at this early hour. If he had to guess, they would set sail soon.

"I'm going to ask who's leaving today and who's taking on passengers," she said. "I'll be back."

As she walked away, his gaze turned back down to the coin purse, which suddenly felt like a bag of rocks he'd once carried out of the mines. He shouldn't accept this—he *couldn't* accept this.

Why is she helping me?

His mind strayed to how she'd felt when she'd been on top of him and how she'd tasted after that. He knew in an instant that he'd never get enough of her. But there hadn't been enough time for them to lose themselves in each other again. Instead, the moment he agreed to accept her help, she'd immediately moved to gather coins hidden around her room and dress them both in nondescript clothes and cloaks.

Why did the idea of leaving hurt so much? None of this made

sense. She was a stranger to him. He should swallow his pride, accept the help, and leave this place behind him.

When she returned a few minutes later to where he hid in the shadows of a nearby alleyway, he said nothing.

"One ship is leaving within the hour," she said. "I bargained down the price somewhat for passage. They are leaving the continent. So, you won't have to worry about finding passage again in the capital. You will, however, have to worry about feeding over the course of the journey. But I suppose, one problem at a time, right?"

She offered a small smile, which he didn't return.

Why couldn't he even act grateful?

It felt like his gut had plummeted into his boots. And his hunger—*fuck*, his hunger was nearly overwhelming. His wrists and neck were no longer covered in blisters, and his stomach twisted and burned with unslaked hunger. Even from where he stood, her scent of strawberries and sunshine was intoxicating. It filled his mouth, his very being, until it consumed his every sense. It was all he could think about—the feel of her blood filling his mouth, drinking her in until it felt like she was all around him. He wanted to get lost in her body, in her blood, to know only *her*.

He began breathing through his mouth again. He mustn't forget that. The sulfurous smells of the bay that connected to the ocean and the smoke coming from chimneys of nearby buildings had given him a false sense of security. And he wouldn't jeopardize her safety. Not after all she'd done for him. It was the least he could do.

"Is something wrong?" Leaning down, she sniffed her cloak, frowning. "Do I smell?"

He cleared his throat, uncertain what to say. He didn't want to sound ungrateful. When he spoke, his voice felt hoarse—as though he'd been screaming for hours.

"It's your blood," he rasped. "I... I don't want to hurt you."

She bit the inside of her cheek, seeming to consider something. But as she opened her mouth to respond, he found his feet moving of their own accord. He must have used his vampire speed because, before he knew what was happening, he'd pulled her into the alley and pressed her against the wall.

She gasped beneath him, her fingers pressing against his chest as she looked up at him, her eyes wide.

But she didn't push him away.

"Fuck, you smell so good," he hissed, feeling the prick of his elongated canines against his lips. Immediately, he tasted his own blood. And between the copper tang of his blood and her scent, it was all he could do to keep himself from ripping out her neck then and there and drinking her dry.

He slammed a fist against the wall behind her before allowing his head to sag.

"Do you need to...?" she began, trailing off.

Was she actually offering herself to him? After everything?

"I..." Words failed him.

Unbidden, he leaned down until his lips brushed against her ear. A growl escaped him, and he felt her shudder beneath him. But instead of pushing him away or telling him to stop, he felt her fingers grip his cloak—as though to pull him closer. As though he wasn't some monster about to unleash himself upon her.

As though she wanted him, too.

The gesture emboldened him, and he leaned down further until his lips hovered above her neck. His breath brushed against her skin even as her heat radiated up to him, inviting him in. Slowly, he pressed his lips against her neck.

It was a single kiss. Gentle and chaste. But it left him feeling feverish, his thoughts growing hazy.

She whimpered beneath him, tilting her head back.

With his vampire abilities, he heard the quickening of her heartbeat and how her breaths came in ragged gasps.

Just one sip. That's it. He would have one last taste of her, and then he'd leave. He'd find a new place to start over, and he'd never see her again.

Slowly, he reached up with a hand and gripped the top of her neck, pulling her head to the side—trapping her in place. His other hand still pressed into the stone building in the alleyway. The shadows of the fading night shrouded them even more than the cloaks they wore as it fought against the rising dawn—and everything that came with it.

"Tell me to stop if I hurt you," he managed past his fangs.

Then he sunk his teeth into her.

She cried out, but the sound wasn't that of pain.

It was pleasure. Pure bliss.

He'd heard her make that very same sound when he'd buried his face in her sweet cunt. As he pulled another draft of her blood into his mouth, he couldn't decide which was the sweeter pleasure —her salty desire or her lifeblood. The taste of her blood was just like her strawberries-and-sunshine scent he found so intoxicating. It was different from the soft richness at her core. But the sounds... oh, the sounds she made were the same. He wanted to hear it again.

His arm slid down from the wall until he wrapped it around her lower back, sinking lower and lower until he found her round ass. And he squeezed, pulling upward. He felt her hands skirt beneath his cloak and shirt. But when her fingernails scraped against his sides, he paused.

Fear sliced through him, and he wondered if he'd hurt her—if she was trying to fight him off in that very moment.

But as he started to pull away, she whispered, "Don't stop."

Instead of returning to her neck, he lowered himself to his knees before her and parted her cloak. Beneath, she wore the black dress of the night before, and he knew from watching her dress in her room that she wore nothing beneath it.

Gently, he pressed one of her legs to the side, and she spread willingly for him. Then he traced kisses up her leg, from her knee, higher and higher until he was a breath away from where he longed to lose himself once more. But instead of licking her pussy that was drenched for him, he did as she asked him—he drank from her once more.

He sunk his fangs into her upper thigh. It was so close to her pussy that he knew her every sense would be heightened as the pleasure of his bite—his venom—filled her. He took a single pull of her blood, and her hand flew to her mouth.

"I'm going to come," she gasped.

Her back arched against the stone wall as she cried out, the sounds barely muffled by the press of the back of her hand against her lips.

When she stilled, he released her leg, his fangs retreating and his hunger only somewhat sated. And then he buried his face in her pussy.

The lingering taste of her blood in his mouth mixing with the heady taste of her desire had him moaning, his cock pressing against his pants. He didn't go as slow as he had only hours ago. Instead, he moved his tongue up and down and plunged his finger into her core. As he did, he reached down to his cock and pulled it free from his pants.

In what felt like moments, they were both coming. His seed splashed against the cobblestones as her body spasmed in pleasure against his face. He wished that moment could last forever, that they didn't have to think about what came next. But they knew they were here on borrowed time.

Then she leaned back, and he did likewise.

For a moment, neither of them moved—their ragged breaths the only sound between them. He looked up at her from where he kneeled, his chest rising and falling, and her eyes locked with his from where she leaned against the wall.

Shaking her head as though to clear her thoughts, she pulled her dress down, closing her cloak and clearing her throat. He tucked his cock back into his pants and stood.

He towered over her and watched as she chewed on her lower lip. Not for the first time, he longed to know just what was on her mind.

Clearing her throat, she said, "Good luck, Rowan."

She turned to leave, but he grabbed her wrist. "Wait."

He knew he should let her go. There was nothing more he could ask of her. There was nothing more he *should* ask of her. She'd already given so much.

"Come with me."

The words were out before he realized what was happening.

Lines formed between her red brows, but she shook her head. "I can't."

"Do you have a reason to stay in Shadowbank?" he dared to ask. Could she have a lover here? Had she lain with him even with another partner in the picture?

When she shook her head, he forged ahead, unable to stop now that the words were out. "Let's find whatever is next for us off these shores. Let's start a new life together."

She dropped her gaze then, and her voice sounded strangely small. "There's only enough money to pay for one passage." When she looked back at him, he thought her lip trembled.

"Then let's speak to the authorities here," he said, knowing the sudden desperation he felt leached into his voice. "We can report Jonas to them."

She shook her head.

"The enchantresses will kick you out the moment they learn you're a vampire," she said. "They'd close the House of Obscurities as punishment for the auctions and imprison Trista and many others. I'd have no job and no place to live, and neither would you. Besides, I wouldn't place my trust in the enchantresses again unless I had no other choice."

Did she mean when her husband left her? Had she gone to them for help before?

There really were no good options for them.

If he stayed, Jonas would find him and take him back—likely throw him into the handcuffs and collar to punish him for what he'd done. Maybe he'd be auctioned tonight regardless of whether he was still a virgin. For the first time, he thought to wonder what Jonas would do to *her* if he found out she was the one who'd taken his virginity. He'd never tell Jonas, but the male had a way of finding things out.

Something like fear iced Rowan's veins at the thought of Jonas laying his hands on Nemera.

If they reported Jonas to the enchantresses, maybe they'd kick Jonas and the troupe out, but Rowan would be forced to leave as well once they realized he was a vampire. And there simply wasn't enough money for him and Nemera to travel by ship together.

"I don't want to leave you."

The words fell from his lips as he leaned forward, pressing his forehead to hers. And damn him, he meant it.

He felt her hands curl into his cloak.

Suddenly, he caught the metallic scent of blood, and he realized he'd forgotten to breathe through his mouth. Glancing down, he spotted blood trickling from where his fangs had punctured her neck.

He felt his pupils shift, his gaze going in and out of focus on that bead of scarlet as it rolled down her neck and onto her collarbone. He swallowed thickly before licking his lips.

I just fed, he thought. *I shouldn't be craving her like this again.*

But his fangs were once again out, unbidden, and all logic slipped from him like sand between his fingers. There was nothing but that trickle of blood and the scent of strawberries and sunshine. Some part of him recognized that scent, but it didn't matter. Not when there was a willing body beneath him. Not when there was *blood.*

"Rowan—" came a voice, but the sound was distant as he grabbed the wrists of his prey in a single hand, locking them in place. With his other hand, he gripped the neck of the squirming little female.

Then he unleashed himself on her.

His fangs sunk into her, and he pulled blood into his mouth.

It was decadent and rich, and it reminded him of rolling fields and summer winds. He drank and drank, feeling her tremble beneath him and pull against his grip on her wrists. But she couldn't move. She was a weak prey—easy to restrain and *feast* on.

As he continued to drink, he distantly heard her cry out in pleasure. She moaned, thrusting her hips against his leg. After the fifth time she cried out, she'd slowly stopped moving. His stomach was full with her blood, but he didn't want to stop. Not now, not ever.

"Please, Rowan," came the voice, weaker now. "I can't come again. It hurts."

He blinked.

He knew that voice.

Immediately, he released her, stumbled backward across the alleyway until he crashed into the opposite wall. His palms scraped against the stones of the building.

Disgust roiled in his gut as he watched Nemera wipe tears away, pressing fingers to her neck. Where he'd bitten her—right above the necklace he'd given her only hours before. Her eyes were rounded with surprise. Was that fear he saw as well? But before he could truly see the emotions rolling over her features, she turned from him and pull the hood of her cloak up.

"I'm sorry," he rasped. "I... I couldn't control it. The hunger."

"It's okay," she said. "You haven't fed since I took your chains off. You had to be starving from your body healing..."

He growled. "Stop making excuses for me. You've done nothing but help me, and I hurt you."

"You stopped," she said, and he watched as she swallowed; though the hood of her cloak kept her eyes from view. "That's what matters."

Her skin seemed paler than before, and he wondered if it was the light of the early morning. He doubted it.

She forced a smile and said, "You should go. Before it's too late."

His fingers slackened as something heavy settled in his chest.

She was right. There was nothing for them. Not here or on

other shores. He'd nearly killed her just now. He should leave before he truly hurt her.

In a greater show of strength than he had, she turned on a heel and strode out of the alley without another word.

Please, a distant part of him thought. *Don't leave.*

He wanted to go after her, but what else was there to say? They couldn't both leave Shadowbank, and he suspected she'd given him everything she had. Could he really take the money knowing that? But if he stayed, he'd be cuffed again in those silver chains, and he'd never know the touch of someone who didn't want to use him again. He was immortal now. Did that mean he'd be a slave to humans for the rest of time? He realized now he didn't want to submit to Jonas for a moment longer. He wanted the chance to choose how he spent his days—and who he pleasured with his bite.

He wanted it to be Nemera.

But they'd only been given one night, and he had to be thankful for that.

I can't leave things like this. I must thank her and apologize at the very least.

He'd taken only a step before he heard the voice that haunted his dreams.

"Where is he?" came Jonas' voice outside the dark alleyway. "Tell me now, and perhaps I won't peel the flesh from your bones."

Rowan moved toward the end of the alley on silent footsteps, using his powers without meaning to. Before he turned the corner, he hesitated.

Breathing deeply, he thought he scented Jonas' two vampire guards. And he wondered if they could smell him as well or if Nemera's desire and the smells of the alley and docks covered his scent.

He couldn't overpower Jonas and two seasoned vampires—not with his woeful lack of experience as a vampire and in combat. If he revealed himself and attempted to help Nemera, they would capture him as well as her, and everything she had done for him would be in vain. She would be furious with him, he knew. So, he hesitated, listening.

"Gone," Nemera said, her voice sharper than he'd ever heard it. "He left on a ship this morning."

Why was she lying for him? She should save herself.

There was a sound like a snicker before Jonas said, "You lie."

She started to speak, but Jonas interrupted her. "You're wearing his necklace."

The ringleader's humorless laughs echoed into the alley, and Rowan felt a new fear surge in his chest.

"You fucked him, didn't you?" Jonas said, his voice dangerously low. "He said he'd give that necklace away when he'd bedded a woman for the first time."

Fuck.

Rowan hadn't thought of that when he'd given Nemera the necklace—hadn't thought of the possibility of Jonas seeing it and recognizing it for what it was. He'd only thought of himself and how he wanted to see her wear it. How he'd wanted her to have a piece of him.

"Take me in his place," Nemera said, her voice trembling. "Auction me. Leave Trista and the others at the House out of it. They had nothing to do with this. I might not be as valuable as a vampire, but I suspect that red hair is a selling point. No?"

"You *did* fuck him, you little cunt," Jonas hissed. There was a pause before he added, "Look around, boys. Rowan might still be nearby."

On instinct, Rowan moved down the alley, which opened up to several more branching streets. He used his vampire speed, zipping down one dark street after another until he circled back to the docks. As he did, he noticed people were slowly filtering into the streets. He'd have to be careful he wasn't seen using his vampire abilities—or else they could alert the enchantresses to his presence.

He moved until he was a few alleys down, closest to the

docked ships. Daring a glance outside of the alley, he spotted two blurring shapes moving to Jonas' side.

His guards.

"They were here," said one guard. "They fucked in the alley before he left by the smell of it."

Jonas had a hand locked around Nemera's wrist. The hood of her cloak had fallen back, and her bright red hair was visible from where Rowan stood.

In a flash, Jonas moved and slapped Nemera across the face. She stumbled forward, but his hand on her wrist prevented her from falling.

Rowan's fangs immediately lengthened, and he moved, about to run toward them, when Jonas spoke again.

"You'll buy his freedom with yours," Jonas said. "And I'll make sure to sell you to the worst people of Shadowbank—ones who take pleasure in pain. You'll never see the light of day again."

Then Jonas moved with supernatural speed, hitting Nemera on the head before her body went limp. One guard grabbed her before she could fall to the cobblestones and tossed her over a shoulder as though she weighed no more than a sack of grain. Then they disappeared in a flash of supernatural speed.

Chest heaving, Rowan's heartbeat drummed in his ears.

For long moments, it was all he could do to take one gasping breath after the next as his mind raced.

Somewhere nearby, sailors shouted to hoist the anchor. That they were setting sail.

The bag of coins weighed heavily in his pocked. If he was going to escape on a ship, it would have to be now—before they left port. If he did, he'd never see Nemera again.

If he did, Jonas would sell her at the auction. Tonight.

Chapter Seven

NEMERA

Nemera woke up to the feel of water splashing over her.

Gasping, she spit out some of the liquid, gagging and trying to get a deep breath. Blinking, she glanced around, noting a large bed with dark tapestries on one side of the room and a hearth twice the size of the one in her own room on the opposite end. A carpet of reds, whites, and blacks extended the length of the room, and there was an oak dresser near the bed and another near the door.

The House of Obscurities.

They were back. And in one of the master suites.

At the door, there were two guards who, at the sight of her waking up, left the room and shut the door behind them.

Keeping guard, no doubt.

It was then she realized she was in a copper bathtub in the center of the carpet, and a woman she didn't recognize sat beside her on a stool with a sponge in her hand.

"Welcome back," the woman said. She was dressed in tight acrobatic garb that was white and blue, the color of a cloudless sky. One of the troupe, then.

"Do I have the guards to thank for my... bed?" Nemera asked, trying to blink back the pain thrumming in her skull from when Jonas had knocked her out.

The woman nodded. "I was called up here when they put you in the empty bath. Told to clean you up for tonight."

Glancing toward the window, Nemera noted the sun had risen in the sky. She guessed it was late morning.

Not looking away from the window, she said, "Does anyone know I'm here?"

"No," the acrobat said. "Just me and the guards."

"Good."

She didn't want Trista or the others trying to save her. She'd gotten herself into this mess, and they didn't need to be dragged into it. Even still, a tightness lodged in her throat, and she tried swallowing it back.

The woman washed her in silence for a time, running the sponge over Nemera's skin. The water was infused with oils she couldn't identify, and rose petals floated across the water's surface. Jonas was sparing no expense for her upcoming auction.

Hands ran through Nemera's hair as the woman spoke, "Is he safe?"

Nemera looked up then, eyes locking with the woman's. She was beautiful with large eyes the color of pale blue crystals, and her blonde hair reminded her of stalks of wheat in late summer.

"What's your name?" Nemera asked.

"Elowyn," the female said as she poured water over Nemera's hair. After a moment, she added, "I wasn't a friend of Rowan's. None of us were—not in the ways that mattered. We were all too afraid to stand up to Jonas or the other vampires. I will always hold on to that shame. But I hated the way they treated Rowan... It was despicable."

Nemera couldn't imagine what it must have been like being on the open roads with the constant threat of demon attacks and the never-ending fear of Jonas and the other vampires who could drink them dry if they stepped out of line.

"Is he safe?" Elowyn repeated.

"Yes," Nemera said, thinking of the last moments she'd seen Rowan, pressed against the wall on the opposite side of the alley, his eyes full of fear. Fear for her, she'd realized belatedly. Fear he'd hurt her.

But he'd stayed hidden and avoided Jonas' vampires. He must have gotten on a ship before they'd found him. He had the money she'd given him, and he'd be long gone by now.

The thought she'd never see him again had something inside her chest twisting.

Come with me.

Had he really meant that? Had he actually wanted her to go with him?

It was just the pleasure talking. He couldn't mean it.

But like the fool she was, her bleeding heart got in the way. Once again, she'd given everything up for a *male*. She'd let herself be used. Hell, she'd *asked* Rowan to let her help him. She'd all but asked for what was coming to her.

In a matter of hours, she'd be auctioned away to the most vile humans of Shadowbank.

"Thank you," Elowyn said. "For doing what I couldn't. What none of us dared to. You're braver than all of us."

Nemera laughed humorlessly. "I'm just a woman who never learned her lesson."

"You don't give yourself enough credit." Elowyn put something else in Nemera's hair, running her fingers through Nemera's long, red curls. "You haven't given up fighting. You're one of the rare ones. The demons have stripped most of our humanity—our ability to care for more than our own hides."

Nemera wasn't sure how to respond. She didn't feel like she'd done anything but keep her head down, trying to save up money to start a new life these last few years. She'd felt that this world, her life, had hardened her once soft heart. But Rowan had found his way into her heart in mere hours. She'd found herself daring to hope, daring to want more for him and herself. She'd seen the desperate girl she'd been, abandoned by her husband and her family with no one to turn to and nowhere to go. She couldn't do *nothing.*

And she realized she didn't regret it. Not one moment with Rowan.

You won't be thinking that once the auctions are through, a darker part of her thought. *When dirty hands are all over your body, using you to slake their pleasures, filling you with their seed.*

Maybe she'd be round with child one day—something she'd avoided in her time with her husband. She doubted her owners would give her the medicines she used now to prevent pregnancy. They might even have a breeding kink, eager to create more redheads like her.

"I'd like to help you escape," Elowyn said as she finished cleaning Nemera and held a towel out for her. "It's the least I can do after my inaction with Rowan. Maybe I can get you to—"

"No," Nemera interrupted as she stood, grabbing the towel from Elowyn and wrapping it around her. "I don't want anyone else to get involved. This is my mess, and it ends with me."

She was always going to be trapped in Shadowbank. She was born here, and she was going to die here. It was foolish of her to dare to want to start a new life in this merciless place. She should have known it was pointless to hope.

At least Rowan got away.

At least one of them would get to dream—to dare to want more.

Chapter Eight

NEMERA

Hours later, Nemera was dressed in lace undergarments —a red lacey corset that barely came up over her breasts and underpants that didn't cover her ass.

The patrons would be able to see nearly every inch of her.

Once bought, she'd have fewer rights than the mistresses in the House of Obscurities. They could choose this line of work, and they were paid for their services. After tonight, Nemera's body would be used at the whims of the vile humans of Shadowbank who lurked in the shadows—whenever and with whoever they wanted. She would be raped again and again.

Two of Jonas' vampire guards entered her room hours after the sun had set. It had to be getting close to midnight. The one on the right smiled at her, lips peeling back, as he lazily twirled the shackles in the air.

Fear filled her chest, and her throat tightened.

She couldn't cry now. She refused to let anyone see her fear.

With far more effort than she cared to think about, she shoved down her terror and didn't fight as the two guards placed her wrists and ankles in shackles made of steel. Not the silver ones Rowan had been in. A short chain connected the shackles from one ankle to another. There was no running away from this. She was well and truly trapped. Then the guards pressed a gag between her lips and tied it behind her head.

She was to have no say in what happened next.

Pausing, she spared a glance over her shoulder to Elowyn, who gave her a nod of farewell.

The guards grabbed Nemera's arms and brought her down back hallways that only the staff knew and into the lowest level of the House.

There would be no saying farewell to Trista, and she hoped that the madam wouldn't try to intervene if she was downstairs—for her own sake.

The guards at the door to the basement opened it without a word, letting them in.

The patrons were already gathered in the rows of seats around the circular stage, drinks in hands, masks over their faces to disguise their identities. More stood at the back of the room or lingered near the bar. Nemera held her chin high as she was pulled down the aisle and onto the stage.

Unlike when Rowan was here, there was a stake at the center of the room. She swallowed thickly, but she didn't object or try to fight as she was brought onto the stage. The guards pulled her arms above her head and hooked her shackles into place before turning without a word and leaving the stage.

For several long moments, she stood at the center of the stage, heart pounding so loudly that the sounds of the whispering crowd were temporarily drowned out.

Don't show them your fear. You will find a way to endure this.

But even as she desperately clung to the shreds of her courage, her breaths grew ragged, and she knew her breasts would be heaving, nearly popping out of the corset. And if they did, she doubted Jonas or his men would bother to cover her up. It was all part of the show.

Jonas appeared from the back of the room with his usual vampire guards flanking him. He strode toward the stage, and she watched each of his heavy footsteps in his polished leather shoes that were as fine as his black trousers and embroidered jacket with long coattails. He was the picture of show business.

"Welcome, one and all!" Jonas said as he bounded onto the stage with a wide grin. "I have some unfortunate news," he began, offering a brief scowl in Nemera's direction. It was so quick, she thought she'd imagined it. "My virgin vampire will no longer be available for auction."

Mutters rippled through the audience, and Nemera watched as some patrons leaned toward one another, sharing whispered words.

"But I won't leave you wanting," he continued. "This night, I have a red beauty that is yours for the taking. And she has red hair *everywhere.*"

Blood rushed to Nemera's cheeks, and she bit down on the gag in her mouth. She reminded herself that she'd chosen this to protect Rowan, Trista, and everyone else in the House. This would be the least of her worries. Far more and far worse awaited her this very night.

His words seemed to pacify the patrons, whose mutters slowly quieted as their attention turned back to the stage. Ladies dressed in lacey black gowns lowered gloved hands, and the men fixed their eyes on Nemera, their gazes sweeping up and down her body.

Nemera held her chin even higher, willing hatred into her gaze.

She would not be cowed so easily.

"Let's start our bidding at one hundred marks," Jonas said.

She stiffened. That was more money than she'd earn in a year of work at the House of Obscurities.

Immediately, one hand rose in the back. It was hard to see into the darkness, as the brightest lanterns were situated around the stage, but she thought it was a man who'd placed the bid.

Jonas nodded from where he stood beside her. "Can I get one hundred twenty-five marks?"

Another hand rose. This time, a woman.

"One hundred fifty marks?"

Two hands went up.

"One seventy-five?" Jonas continued without hesitation. When no one raised their hand immediately, he turned toward Nemera. Quiet fury filled his gaze, and he reached up, squeezing her breast painfully.

She cried out, the sound muffled in the gag.

"She's still young and has many years of pleasure to offer you," Jonas said. "She can even double as a maid or bear your children."

The ringleader's eyes skirted down her body to her lacey underwear.

"In case you don't believe it," he began, reaching for the lace at her hips. With the flick of a wrist, he ripped her underwear, and it fell to her feet.

She was bare before the audience—her pussy visible for all to see.

As he'd claimed, the hair on her pussy was red like the hair on her head, though she'd kept it trimmed short. And in that moment, all gazes fell on her, feasting on her cunt with their eyes.

"Surely, this red beauty is worth one hundred seventy-five marks," Jonas said. Then he reached down, cupping her pussy. "Shall I let one of you take her for a test ride?"

Yanking against her chains, she hissed a few curses into the gag, trying to free herself from his touch. But the movements only had his fingers plunging deeper into her. Feeling this, he moved his fingers in a slow, tantalizing circle before removing his hand and showing it to the audience.

"A wanton thing, too."

Despite herself, despite her hatred of Jonas and disgust at being displayed like an animal at market, her body betrayed her.

A man wearing a solid black mask across his eyes and nose stood from his seat toward the middle of the audience. Like Jonas, he wore black trousers and a black jacket. It wasn't as fine a material as the ringleader's, but it was clean and nondescript. Perfect for moving in secret in the dead of night.

"I'll take her for a test ride," the man said, grabbing the bulge in his pants as he strode toward the stage. "If she's as good as you say, perhaps I'll pay your one hundred seventy-five."

Fear sliced through her chest.

No. No, no, no.

This couldn't be happening. She wasn't about to be fucked in front of everyone. Not like this. Surely, they'd wait until they'd purchased her and brought her back to whatever prison she'd be kept in.

Again, Nemera pulled at the cuffs at her wrists, trying to break free of where they'd been locked into the stake above her head. But it was no use. There was nothing she could do as the male approached the stage, lust in his gaze.

Before he could walk up the stairs, the back door to the room banged open, and a voice she'd never dared hope to hear again shouted.

"Two hundred marks."

Gasping, she nearly sobbed.

Rowan stood at the back of the room, the coin purse she'd given him in his fist. It was the exact amount she'd given to him for passage on the ship off the continent. Every coin she'd earned in her years of working at the House of Obscurities. The very coin she'd hoped would afford her a better future either in Shadow-bank or in another place.

His features seemed harder than usual—his eyes narrowed into slits, his back straight beneath the cloak she'd given him, and his jawline sharp enough to cut hearts.

"Look who's returned," Jonas said, his eyes narrowing even as an artificial smile crept over his stiffened features. "I doubt you possess that kind of money." The ringleader offered a placating smile to the patrons, who were once again whispering to each other, growing agitated.

In a flash, Rowan was on the stage, his eyes soaking her in. Worry filled his gaze, raw and sharp. That single look said far more than any words could convey.

"Are you okay?" he whispered to her.

She nodded, tears streaming down her cheeks.

Turning to Jonas, Rowan dropped the coin purse into the ringleader's hands.

No, she thought. *You can't be here. Jonas could capture you. Get out while you still can.*

For a moment, she wondered if he'd accept the money or try to auction them both. Would he risk a scene in front of the patrons and the potential that they may not return—or report the auctions to the enchantresses? For him to have enough money to travel to the next town, he'd need willing patrons with open coin purses. He couldn't afford to be known as the auctioneer who arrested his highest bidder—which, in this instance, was Rowan.

Then she thought to wonder if Jonas had the silver handcuffs. If he did, who would put them on Rowan if he fought them? Would other vampires touch them? Or would they not be able to tolerate the silver?

But if Jonas revealed that there were more vampires than Rowan in the troupe, the patrons would likely be even more tempted to tell the enchantresses—especially when these vampires weren't for sale. These were vampires who could feed on them. And Jonas would have to use his own vampire abilities to capture Rowan if he chose to fight. His guards would likely get pulled into the fight.

Would he take that risk?

As long moments ticked by, no one moved toward them.

Wordlessly, Jonas counted the money. Looking up, he nodded, the veins in his jaw bulging as he did.

"Sold," he said to the patrons, who muttered in displeasure, many standing to leave.

Leaning in, Jonas whispered loudly enough that only Nemera and Rowan could hear, "I will get back at you both for this. Mark my words."

Rowan stood his ground, his narrowed eyes filled with a

menace she'd never seen before. For a moment, she wondered if he would attack the ringleader then and there.

"She belongs to me," Rowan hissed.

In a flash of movement, Rowan released her cuffs from the stake. As she dropped her arms, blood rushed into them, and her knees buckled. Before she could collapse, Rowan caught her, pulling her into his arms and walking off the stage. As he strode toward the exit, Trista intercepted them, a key in her fist. She removed the cuffs from Nemera's wrists and ankles.

"Run," Trista whispered. "Leave Shadowbank, and never look back. I'll buy you as much time as I can."

There was only enough time to reach out and squeeze her hand in farewell before there was a flash of movement and the House of Obscurities was gone.

Even as Rowan moved unnaturally fast with his vampire abilities, a single thought went through her mind.

Rowan hadn't abandoned her. He'd come back.

She'd been auctioned to a vampire.

Now, she was his, and he was hers. Until Jonas caught up with them.

Chapter Nine

ROWAN

Rowan ran until he lost track of the number of turns he made, the surrounding buildings a mere blur. Skidding to a stop, he carried Nemera into a darkened alley that smelled of stale bread and rotten fruit.

The night would give way to dawn in a few hours. People wouldn't begin to emerge from their homes just yet.

Gently, he placed her down, watching as her legs wobbled before she steadied herself with a hand against the wall. She was naked from the waist down, and he quickly pulled his shirt over his head. It had been one she had taken from the same colleague she'd borrowed the cloak from.

Reaching out, he offered it to her, and she accepted.

Luckily, it was large and covered her. He also offered her the cloak, which dragged on the ground after she donned it. While he was recognizable enough to Jonas' men, Nemera's hair would be a red beacon that could be identified from afar.

"Are you okay?" he asked as he pulled up the hood, tucking her hair in.

Slowly, she nodded. "You shouldn't have come. Now, neither of us can afford passage on a ship, and Jonas will find us both soon."

Even with his vampire powers, the two of them alone—without supplies, weapons, or proper clothes and shoes—wouldn't stand a chance traveling on foot to one of the closest cities. The demons would devour them as soon as they stepped outside of Shadowbank's ward. It had been a miracle the troupe had made it this far. So many vampires had died defending the troupe.

"I couldn't leave you," he said honestly.

Guilt washed over him. Not only had he spent all of Nemera's savings, but now she was in danger, too. They may not survive until dawn.

She sighed, running a hand over her hood. "The ships will be gone by now. It could be weeks until the next ones arrive, even if we could afford passage." She shook her head. "I'm so tired, I can't think straight."

They hadn't slept the night before, and this would be their second night without rest.

Gesturing toward the deeper shadows of the alley—where the strongest smells were coming from—he said, "Perhaps we should rest. We won't be of any use if we are exhausted."

The smells would hopefully be enough to keep Jonas' vampire guards off his and Nemera's scent.

Nodding, she strode past burlap sacks of what must be rotten potatoes and other piles of garbage to the back of the alley, and he followed her. She sunk down until she sat, leaning against a wall. She seemed so small, so vulnerable in this light, curled up as she was.

Some instinct swelled inside of him, and he knew then he wanted to protect her for however long she let him.

It was then he realized he'd brought them to the more remote houses against the outer wall surrounding the village, nearest the looming forest.

Lowering himself, he sat a few feet away from her, not wanting to touch her—worried just what fears must be going through her mind after having Jonas display her in that way. He didn't want to make it worse. He didn't want to scare her. But as the minutes stretched on and his eyelids grew heavy, he blinked awake at the sound of chattering teeth. Belatedly, he realized she was shivering and had wrapped the cloak tightly around her thin frame.

His heart sunk. "I wish I could offer you my body's warmth. But I'd only make you colder."

Fall had settled over the land, and the nights grew colder. Even with his shirt and cloak, it was woefully insufficient to keep her warm.

"It's fine," she said. "I'm f-fine."

Brows drawing together, he wasn't sure what to say. There was nothing he could do or say to make any of this better. But she saved him the need to speak when she spoke again.

"C-can I put my head on your lap?"

The words warmed something in his chest, and he nodded, lowering his legs until they were stretched out before him.

She moved to him before settling her head on his lap and closing her eyes. To his surprise, it wasn't long until her shivers slowed and she slipped into the land of dreams. As his own eyes grew heavy, a single thought ran through his mind.

She didn't use me. She's not like my father or Jonas. She's different.

Then exhaustion took him.

THE NEXT MORNING, Rowan awoke to the feel of Nemera reaching for him, her fingers wrapping around his where they rested on her stomach.

She lay on her back, features slack in sleep and her head nestled in his lap. Even with the dew of the early morning dusting across their bodies and the floor of the alley, he didn't want to move. He didn't want to disturb her sleep. She looked so peaceful, but he noted the purple hue of her lips and knew they had to find a place for them to clean up and get warm. But where?

Running his free hand over her hair, he said, "Nemera. Wake up."

She grumbled, brows drawing together as she rolled onto her side, not letting go of his hand.

"We need to find clothes and something for you to eat," he said, marveling at her beauty—that she was alive and here. That he got to see her again. "And we need to get you warm so you don't get sick."

Slowly, she rose to a seated position and looked around. Then she turned to look at him. Her dark eyes flicked between his as though searching for something, though he wasn't sure what.

Then she stood, and he did likewise. Securing the cloak over her hair, she strode out of the alley.

"Let's look for the nearest inns or taverns," she said over a shoulder. "But don't hold your breath. They turned me away in the past. I doubt anything has changed."

She was right.

They walked into three inns, each of which had taverns and a common room on the main floor. Patrons were sitting down to breakfast, and the smell of eggs and potatoes wafted to them. But as soon as they spotted Nemera's red hair beneath her cloak, they turned her away.

"Your husband owes a hundred marks," one barkeep said, waving a serving spoon at them. "Come back when you have the money to pay off his debts."

"I'm no longer with him. He left years ago," Nemera said, but they wouldn't listen.

Both he and Nemera were unceremoniously ushered out the front door before it was closed behind them.

Sighing, Nemera turned, her eyes cast on the cobblestone streets.

"Maybe if I threaten to rip out his throat, he'd recall his manners," he growled.

"Don't," she said. "He's not worth it."

"Fine." He gestured down the street to another inn. "Let's try another. Maybe we'll have better luck."

Than the last three.

She sunk down onto the front step to the inn. "Why bother? We'll just be turned away. It's like how it was years ago. No one would give me work. They wouldn't even listen to me. All anyone cared about was what my husband owed them."

"I'll make them listen," he said, a surge of protectiveness filling him. She needed food, clothes, and a place to warm up. Reaching out, he looped an arm through one of hers, gently pulling her to her feet. "Come on."

She didn't object but followed him to the next inn. Pushing the doors open, he guided them inside into the dark common room. It was smaller than the others they'd seen, but there were half a dozen people sitting down to break their fasts. Before he could ask the innkeeper for a room or breakfast, there was a hand on his back.

Instinctively, he released Nemera's arm and turned, pushing her behind him, putting himself between her and whatever came for them.

Had Jonas and his guards found them already?

But when he turned, he was surprised by the sight of one of the troupe. Elowyn, he thought her name was.

She simply nodded to him before walking past them to the innkeeper.

"One room for the night," Elowyn said, passing payment. "And meals."

The man nodded and offered her a room key. "Up the stairs in the back. Second floor. Third door on the right."

Elowyn strode toward where the innkeeper had indicated, and Rowan didn't miss the scowl he directed Nemera's way. But the man didn't stop them as they walked across the common room and up the stairs.

Unlocking the door and holding it wide, Elowyn gestured for

them to go inside. It was then that Rowan noticed she had a bag slung over a shoulder.

Without a word, he strode inside, holding Nemera's hand as they walked into the dark room. Elowyn closed the door before going to the hearth and lighting it.

"Jonas' guards are looking for you," Elowyn said as she stoked the small flames.

Nemera strode over to the hearth, settling herself onto the ground before it and extending her hands toward the fire.

"I collected enough money from the other performers who wanted to help, but it's not enough for you both to leave by ship," Elowyn said, turning to him. "I'm afraid it's only enough for this room for a night, food, and some clothes."

Rowan's eyes narrowed. "Why are you helping us?"

"We should have helped you all along," Elowyn said, dropping a bag on the bed. "This is the least we can do." She paused, her brows drawing together. "I'm sorry I didn't help you before."

Striding over to him, she placed the room key in his hand, closing his fingers around it. Without another word, she left the room, the crackling fireplace the only sound after she closed the door.

Rowan had expected no one to help him when he'd been under Jonas' control. There were too many dangers on the road. Jonas would have left any performer who dared to speak up behind, leaving them to the demons that were sure to emerge. Sure, he'd longed for someone to stand up for him, but he'd never expected it.

He wasn't sure what to make of Elowyn's actions.

Walking to the bed, he opened the bag to reveal a female's trousers, boots, bodice, and a long-sleeved top. There were also a male's leather boots, trousers, and a shirt with laces. There weren't cloaks for both of them, but they had his. It would drag along the ground when Nemera wore it and it wouldn't keep her warm in the nights if they had to sleep outside again, but it would have to be enough for now.

"She was kind to me before the auction," Nemera said quietly. "She wanted to know that you were okay, and she offered to help me escape."

Looking back at Nemera, he noted a distance in her eyes that hadn't been there before as she stared into the flames, her face devoid of expression.

Going over to her, he lowered himself beside her. The flames of the hearth flickered more strongly now, and he could feel the heat radiating off them.

"What is it?" he asked. "Have I done something?"

Of course, you have, he thought. *Last time she saw you, you nearly ripped out her throat.*

"I should apologize for what happened in the alley," he added hurriedly. "I never should have lost control in the way I did. And I should have come after you. As soon as you disappeared, I knew I'd made the worst mistake of my life."

Blinking, she turned and looked up at him, surprise in her eyes.

"It's what you are, Rowan. You don't have to apologize for needing to feed. And you stopped. That's what matters. But I didn't expect you to come after me. I offered myself willingly in your place. I..." She turned back to the flames, the strange emptiness returning to her eyes. "I wanted you to be happy."

"Then what is it?" he asked, longing to touch her, to wrap his arm around her, but he kept his arms at his sides, uncertain whether the touch would be welcome.

As soon as the words were out, he wanted to smack himself. She'd just lost her life at the House of Obscurities, her job, and it was all his fault. She had to be devastated.

"Him." She wrapped her arms around her knees, pulling them to her chest. "He's always going to haunt me in this town. I'm never going to find another job. My ex-husband has soured so many relationships, and everyone here is always going to associate me with him. Because of him, we're going to die when winter sets in—or I am. That's if Jonas doesn't kill us in the coming days."

For long moments, Rowan said nothing, allowing her words to sink in.

"Can I touch you?" he said at last.

When she nodded, he scooted toward her and wrapped his arms over her shoulders and the damp cloak. To his surprise, she leaned into him, resting her head in the crook of his neck.

"We're going to get through this," he said. "Things might seem bleak now, and perhaps they are. But we will survive this. We will find a way to keep a roof over our heads. If I have to work for us both, I will. Gladly. If it means having you in my life and safe, it's worth it."

She shook her head. "I don't want you to feel you have to work on my behalf like what you had to do for your father. I want to help."

His throat tightened at the thought of his father, of the prison he'd been locked in without knowing it.

"You're not my father," he said. "I want to protect you. Please... Let me take care of you."

For a moment, there was only the rise and fall of her shoulders as she breathed, still leaning into him.

"We can't risk anyone finding out what you are," she said. "The longer you're around people, the greater the risk that you might... lose control."

She had a point. A very valid one. The moment his fangs appeared, unbidden, he would be kicked out of Shadowbank.

"I'll learn to control it," he said with more confidence than he felt.

"There isn't time for you to practice," she said. "Not when we need a job now—somewhere to sleep and food for me."

He held her tightly against him, wishing he could remove the fears that plagued her mind. "We'll find a way. One day at a time, we'll figure this out. I promise."

She trembled beneath him, and it took him a moment to realize she was crying. He held her there in front of the fire, holding her close, letting her mourn the life she'd had until her cloak was dry.

Eventually, she fell asleep, and he carried her to bed, removing the cloak before tucking her into the blankets. He settled himself into a chair beside the window, glancing out through the glass panes at the lowering sun as the hours of the day ticked by too quickly.

He'd meant what he said.

He would protect her, even if it cost him his life.

Chapter Ten

ROWAN

The next morning, Rowan and Nemera bathed and dressed in their new clothes, preparing to leave. Earlier, he'd brought up a large tray of food and watched with pleasure as Nemera ate. She needed her strength for whatever came next.

Somehow, they'd have to avoid Jonas. At least, just long enough until he left Shadowbank for the next village.

As they strode through the common room, he paused as he caught conversations from nearby tables.

"Another person has gone missing," one man said from a nearby table before biting into a biscuit.

"That's the fifth one in the last few days," said the woman across from him.

A server appeared at their table, pouring them fresh cups of tea. "I heard it was closer to ten."

"*Ten* people have gone missing?" the first man said through his biscuit. "How can the enchantresses let this happen? Could demons have gotten through the ward?"

Ahead of him, Nemera pushed through the front door, and Rowan hurried after her.

It was mid-morning, and people were moving about—pulling

wagons, guiding ponies with large saddlebags, or carrying their own goods. Nemera pulled up the hood of her cloak, keeping her head low as she walked up the cobblestone streets.

"Where should we go?" he asked, knowing he'd have to rely on her knowledge of this village and hating he couldn't do more.

They'd strode down several streets, and he wondered where they were headed.

Before she could respond, there was a flash of movement, and he pulled her into a nearby alley.

Somehow, he'd pressed her against the stone wall of a building, his arms bracketing on either side of her, shielding her with his body.

The movement had been quick—too quick for any human—and we wondered if it had been one of Jonas' vampires. When no one followed them into the alley, he slowly stepped back from Nemera and strode to the opening of the alley, glancing up and down the streets. He didn't spot any of Jonas' vampires, but that didn't mean they weren't nearby.

The wind stirred the stale air of the alley, and he caught Trista's scent. But he didn't move. Instead, he pressed his back to the alley wall, grabbing Nemera's hand on instinct. While Trista had said she'd help them at the auction, it was possible Jonas had forced her to help him and his guards in their search for Rowan and Nemera.

As Trista walked past the alley, not turning toward them, Nemera's eyes lit up.

"Trista!" Nemera called, pulling her hand free of his and running toward the alley's entrance.

"Wait," he began, but she'd already crossed the alley.

It could be a trap. And if it was, his little human had run right into it with both arms open as she hugged Trista.

"Thank goodness I found you first," Trista said, passing a bag to Nemera. "I have cloaks, blankets, and some food. It isn't much, but it's something."

"Thank you," Nemera said, relief shining in her eyes.

In a flash, he stood beside her, pulling both females into the alley and eyeing the bright streets.

"Of course," Trista said. "You're one of mine, child."

"What happened since we left?" Nemera asked.

Trista chewed on her lip before saying, "It's bad. There are a lot of vampires now. Even more than when the troupe came here. I think Jonas has been turning people in Shadowbank."

"That explains the disappearances," he said before explaining what he'd heard at the inn that morning.

"Maybe it's time we bring in the enchantresses," Nemera said. "I hate to ask for their help, but only they're powerful enough to stop Jonas and his vampires. Especially if he's building a small army. Come with us, Trista. If you're honest with them about what's been happening, I'm sure they will grant you leniency. They may not close the House either."

Rowan frowned. "And if they don't?"

Trista sighed. "The cost of hosting auctions is a lifetime of imprisonment."

He knew he should be angry with Trista for hosting auctions —one that had nearly taken both his and Nemera's freedoms away and forced them into a life of servitude. But he didn't have the energy to hold a grudge. He needed to keep Nemera safe, and they needed to get away from Jonas.

"Alright. I'll come with you," Trista said as she turned and strode from the alley and back into the street. Before she'd taken two steps, there was a flash of movement.

The first thing he registered was the sight of a metal blade poking through Trista's abdomen. Next, he watched, as though in slow motion, blood flow from the wound and pour onto the ground. Instantly, his fangs pressed into his lips, and hunger burned through him, making all other thoughts a distant memory.

Somewhere behind him, Nemera screamed.

One of Jonas' vampires came into view of the alley, a feral smile on his lips as he yanked on his blade. There was a wet squelch, and he pulled the blade free before Trista's body dropped to the ground. Dead instantly.

"I knew she'd lead us to you," Jonas' guard said.

On instinct, Rowan turned, scooping Nemera into his arms. She fought him at first, her fists hitting his shoulder as she called for Trista. But Jonas' guard directed the sword at Nemera. There wasn't time to mourn the madam now. It was flee or die. So, he raced out of the alley and through the streets with Nemera in his arms, dodging between buildings, humans, and carts. He didn't bother to disguise his vampire speed. There wasn't time for caution—not with Jonas' guard on their heels. But even with steps faster than any human, the vampire was right behind them. He was far more experienced than Rowan and knew how to use his vampire powers.

If they didn't lose him, and soon, they were done for.

"Turn left," Nemera called over the whooshing of the wind as they sped over cobblestones, parallel to the three-story wall that surrounded the entire village.

He didn't ask questions. He just moved.

She shouted a series of directions, and as he followed, he felt the vampire behind him slow.

"Stop!" she called, and he skidded to a halt.

Nemera leaped out of his arms, sprinting for the large stone building before them. It was several stories tall—as tall as the wall beside it. She strode up to massive round oak doors and pounded a fist. Before anyone inside could respond, two enchantresses appeared from down the street in black leather. Two crossing swords were at the back of the taller enchantress, but there were more knives and blades than he could count on them both.

"Enchantresses!" Nemera shouted, waving her hand. "Help us! Please!"

Hearing the fear in Nemera's voice, both females sped down the street and closed the distance quickly.

With his vampire abilities, he heard Jonas' guard stop a few buildings away, lurking in the shadows. The moment the enchantresses appeared, he turned and fled in the opposite direction.

They were safe—for now.

Between gasping breaths and tears, Nemera revealed the events of the last few days to the enchantresses, though she was careful not to mention that Rowan was a vampire.

The one called Jessamine looked at Arabella, an eyebrow raised.

"A couple of vampires would be easy," Jessamine said, speaking to Arabella as though they weren't here. "It's your call."

Rowan placed a hand on Nemera's shoulder, pulling her behind him. Vampires were forbidden in Shadowbank, but would Nemera be in danger by associating with him? He'd shield her from these powerful females if he must.

Even though he couldn't sense her power like magic wielders, he could tell by the easy shift of her muscled shoulders and the way she held herself that this was a female accustomed to making decisions—and having others listen to them without question. That kind of authority was only given to those with power, and significant power at that.

Perhaps she was powerful enough to stop Jonas.

Arabella's eyes narrowed as she watched his movement. "Easy. You're safe with us."

"There may be more vampires," he said. "We heard people talking about disappearances earlier. Trista believed Jonas was turning people."

Jessamine's narrowed eyes shifted from Rowan to Nemera and then back to Arabella as though seeing what wasn't said. "There have been an unusual number of people going missing the last few days. If it's new vampires in a feeding frenzy, it could become serious. Should we bring attention to this...?"

Arabella's eyes fell on Rowan, sweeping over him before looking at Nemera. Was that guilt he saw in the enchantress' gaze? That wasn't possible.

"Not yet." With a jerk of her chin, Arabella gestured to the roads from which he and Nemera had come. "Get Brynne and Cora. Be discreet, Jessamine. Have them care for Trista's body. Wait for me to send word. I'll look into this myself."

Nodding, Jessamine's hand rested casually on the blade at her hip. "What about you?"

Arabella's gaze flicked to Rowan, eyebrow raised. "We have a date with a ringleader."

Chapter Eleven

NEMERA

When Jessamine disappeared around the curve in the road, Arabella turned to them. "Come with me."

Nemera and Rowan followed the enchantress down several streets until they stopped in an alcove in a curve in the three-story stone wall that surrounded Shadowbank that Nemera didn't even know existed. It appeared to be a training area with an open, flat grassy area in the curve of the wall. It was entirely secluded, far from nearby buildings, and eavesdropping would be impossible. Anyone trying to listen in would have to approach them head-on since there was nowhere to hide. It was only wall and grass. Above them, there were no guards along the wall.

Spinning on a heel, Arabella turned to face them. "Tell me."

Nemera frowned. "Tell you what?"

"The full truth," the enchantress said.

Just what did she mean by that?

Nemera considered her next words carefully. It was clear Arabella knew they weren't telling her everything. She likely suspected Rowan. If she knew about him, would she kick him out of Shadowbank that very day? That was a risk she couldn't take.

"We did tell you," Nemera began, but Arabella cut her off, waving a hand.

"I know bullshit when I smell it," Arabella said. "There's something else you're not telling me."

Nemera bit the inside of her cheek. Was it too much to hope that Arabella and the enchantresses would take care of Jonas and the other vampires and leave Rowan out of it?

When Nemera didn't immediately open her mouth to speak, the enchantress turned to Rowan. "How did you come to join Jonas' troupe? Why aren't you with them now?"

"I..." Rowan began but stopped to clear his throat, clearly as uncertain as Nemera how to proceed. "I fell for Nemera."

"Mhm," Arabella said, crossing her arms. "And the fangs?" She nodded to Nemera's neck—and the bite marks she'd completely forgotten to cover.

"Jonas," Nemera lied, interjecting before Rowan could. "He fed on me before the auction."

Arabella raised an eyebrow.

Nemera's heart slammed in her chest. She'd only just gotten Rowan back. She couldn't lose him. Not again. Did she dare tell Arabella the truth? The enchantress didn't believe a word they'd said. However, she'd gone out of her way to speak with Nemera and Rowan without Jessamine. Was it all a ruse to get more information out of them? Or was she trying to keep information from the others? Was she trying to keep what Rowan was—what she suspected he was—a secret?

"Once, you came to me for help," Arabella said, her gaze fixed on something in the distance. "Your husband had gambled your home away, and I did nothing. I've regretted it every day since." Her gaze turned back to Nemera. "I'd like to make up for that now."

Nemera started.

That day was why she had lost faith in the enchantresses.

Years ago, she'd sought an audience with the head enchantress at the Quarter, the stronghold of the enchantresses, hoping to save her home. Arabella had been there when she'd spoken with Iris—standing at her shoulder and saying nothing. The head enchantress had said property ownership wasn't their domain. If her husband had lost their home, then there was nothing the enchantresses could do. They presided over the safety of the village, not the politics of it.

Nemera had no magical ability, no reason she could join the enchantresses' ranks. So, she'd been sent away—homeless, jobless, and without a shred of hope.

"It wasn't your call," Nemera said, blinking back the tears that threatened to spill over.

"Perhaps not, but I obeyed it. And you slept on the streets because of it." Arabella nodded to Rowan. "Is he a vampire?"

For a long moment, Nemera considered whether to lie. But it would come out, eventually. Without the experience to control his thirst, it was only a matter of time before Rowan revealed what he was. Perhaps she could use Arabella's guilt.

"Yes," Nemera said. "And he's with me."

Arabella nodded. "I thought as much. You two seem smitten." Sighing, she pinched the bridge of her nose with her thumb and forefinger. "All magic wielders can sense each other. Where I go, any enchantresses who are nearby can feel my magic."

Nemera frowned. "Why are you telling me this?"

"You want Jonas gone. So do I," Arabella said. "I won't let the bastard hurt anyone else in my village. But you want Rowan to stay in Shadowbank. Is that right?"

"Yes..."

Arabella crossed her arms, her leathers tightening around her muscled biceps. "Then that means we can't let the head enchantress know what we are up to. The more enchantresses there are, the more likely we will draw her attention. Any magic wielder would sense a group of enchantresses from streets away— it would feel like the earth before a thunderstorm with so much magic in one place. And the minute the head enchantress gets involved, she'll suspect what Rowan is."

And he'll be kicked out of Shadowbank.

"We?" Nemera dared to ask.

Arabella nodded. "We."

"What do you propose?" Rowan shifted at Nemera's side, drawing closer as though to shield her from the enchantress.

"To start? Asking Jonas to leave. Nicely," Arabella said. "One of his vampires saw you approaching us. They'll know I'm helping you. So, we'll talk to him together. Hopefully, he's as eager to leave town as we are to have him go."

"And if he doesn't agree to leave?" Nemera asked.

"Or tries to kill Nemera or I on sight?" Rowan added.

Arabella's hand settled on a blade at her hip. "One problem at a time. Let's just hope he plays nice—and we don't need backup."

NEMERA'S HEART pounded as she glanced around the corner of a building, eyeing the front door of the House of Obscurities.

They don't know, she thought. *No one inside knows Trista is dead.*

But everyone who worked in the House would know soon— once Jonas was taken care of.

Arabella and Rowan stood beside her, waiting for her to take the first step.

Taking a breath, she stepped forward, but Rowan caught her wrist. Looking up, her eyes connected with his, and there was a flurry of emotions swirling in them. Was that fear she saw? Brows drawing together, he leaned down. For a moment, she thought he'd kiss her.

She hadn't forgotten that, even after everything they'd done, their lips hadn't touched yet. Her heart fluttered, and she closed her eyes. But rather than the feel of his lips against hers, she felt a gentle press on her forehead.

Blinking, she stood for a long moment as Rowan took a step back and said, "Be careful."

Had he just kissed her forehead? The thought of it had something melting inside her chest.

"You, too," she said and then strode out into the street—with an enchantress and a vampire on her heels.

How had she gone from a human woman who lived a quiet married life in the village to someone who was facing down vampire ringleaders and befriending magic wielders and immortals? Somehow, her life had gone completely awry. Yet, she couldn't find it in her to regret anything—not if it meant that she'd meet Rowan.

As she walked, her thoughts raced.

There was a chance Jonas' guards would kill her or Rowan on sight. But she didn't think they'd kill her in the street where anyone could see, and certainly not with an enchantress there. No, they'd grab her when no one was around, pull her into a darkened corner of the brothel or an empty alleyway, have a vampire drain her dry, and dump her body.

But they killed Trista so openly, a distant part of her thought.

Best not to think on that now.

There would be time to mourn Trista later.

With as much confidence as Nemera could muster, she strode through the center of the cobblestone streets and through the front door. Walking up to the bar, she spotted one of her colleagues cleaning goblets, and she said, "We're here to talk to Jonas."

The man's eyes drew wide, and she wondered if he'd been there the night she'd been auctioned. He managed a nod before disappearing down a back hallway.

Nemera settled into a nearby table beside Arabella and Rowan.

Unable to sit back or force the pretense of a calm demeanor, she leaned forward, heels bouncing. Long fingers wrapped around hers, and she looked up to see Rowan offering her a reassuring smile as he held her hand in his.

A few minutes later, Jonas appeared with two of his vampire

guards flanking him. One was the vampire who had been chasing them. The one who'd run Trista through. Was there blood on his blade even now?

To the average person's eye, the three males wouldn't appear to be vampires—not without seeing their fangs. All three seemed to have mastered their bloodlust, and elongated canines didn't press past their lips. To most, Jonas and his guards would appear like a human ringleader and two typical guards—hired swords with more muscles than brains.

"Welcome," Jonas said, sweeping his arms widely and smiling —as though he owned the place.

Nemera's eyes narrowed, but she and Rowan didn't speak as Jonas settled into a chair across from them. Behind him, his guards stood, hands crossed in front of them. Meanwhile, Arabella lounged back in her chair as though she hadn't a care in the world. As though three vampires who wanted to kill them hadn't just entered the room.

Was the enchantress really that powerful that three vampires were of no concern? Nemera knew she was second-in-command to the head enchantress, but she'd never truly imagined just what kind of magic this female must have access to in order to have gained that sort of power in the Circle.

"To what do I owe this visit?" Jonas asked as he picked a nonexistent piece of lint from his jacket. As always, he was immaculately dressed as though, at any moment, he could be called onto the stage. His jacket was free of wrinkles, and his black pants were perfectly tailored.

"I'm making my rounds to inns with guests from out of town," Arabella said, wearing a bored expression. "Making sure everyone is aware of the rules of our village."

"Oh?" Jonas said. "And what rules are those?"

Leaning forward, Arabella rested her elbows on the table. "The usual. No thievery, auctions, assault, rape, murder, or violence of any kind. Oh, and no vampires." Her last words, she added almost as though they were an afterthought. "Anyone who commits crimes in Shadowbank must also face the consequences.”

Jonas pressed a hand to his chest as though preparing to utter an oath—out his ass, no doubt. “I’m an honest businessman. I nor my people would ever take part in any of the sort.”

“I’m glad to hear it,” Arabella said, her eyes locked on his. “I’d hate to escort anyone out of Shadowbank—or to the dungeons. It’d ruin my whole day.”

The dry sarcasm in the enchantress’ tone was so surprising that Nemera nearly laughed. She’d only known the female to be the serious type. Biting her lip, Nemera narrowly suppressed a smile as Jonas’ eyes narrowed.

“I also have to ask,” Arabella continued. “When do you intend to leave town?”

It was Jonas’ turn to lean back in his chair. “Hard to know.” His eyes flicked to Rowan. “I lost a great deal of money recently.” Slowly, he shifted his gaze back to Arabella. “I need to make up the gap to afford travel to the next village. I might linger for a while yet. Besides, I hear the House of Obscurities might be under new ownership.” The final words he spoke directly to Nemera.

Molten anger burned through her, and she pushed to her feet.

“Murderer,” she hissed. “You’re a heartless, despicable murderer.”

Arabella’s hand was at her arm, and Rowan leaned forward in his seat. Only Jonas and his guards seemed unaffected by her outburst.

“That’s a serious allegation, girl,” Jonas said, his eyes flickering with delight. He’d achieved what he’d sought—to get under her skin. But why?

“Perhaps I’ll make an investment in this village,” Jonas continued, his eyes locking with hers. “Perhaps the House will be under new management soon. And if I take over, trust that you’ll never be welcome here ever again. After your little stunt, I’ll make certain you never find work in Shadowbank.”

Releasing Nemera’s arm, Arabella’s head tilted back as she

laughed. "You've got a pair of tits on you. I'll give you that. You're as bold as many enchantresses I've trained. But brashness won't solve all your problems. And I intend to make myself one if you don't leave soon. Quietly. I'm aware of your business here. Leave today before my order gets involved. And touch another person from my village, make any more of your little vampires, and you'll wish you never stepped foot here."

Slowly, Nemera sank back into her seat, never taking her eyes off the ringleader.

Jonas sighed heavily as though he were about to deliver bad news. "I wish I could, Enchantress. I do. But as I said before, I lost a great deal of money here. In order to afford to continue my current business, I need to make up the difference."

"What will it take for you to leave?" Rowan asked, which had the ringleader's attention shifting to him, eyes hungry.

For a long moment, Jonas said nothing, only studying Rowan. His eyes skirted lower, lingering on his chest—where Rowan's necklace would have been. The necklace that Nemera now wore.

"You," Jonas said. "Return to your place by my side, and I'll gladly leave this backwater village behind. You might not be a virgin any longer, but I daresay a handsome face like that would... draw a crowd."

"You can't expect me to—" Arabella began, but Rowan cut her off.

"And you'll leave Nemera alone? Neither you nor your people will harm her?"

Jonas placed a hand over his heart atop his embroidered jacket. "On my honor as a businessman. She won't be touched."

"She's mine," Rowan said. "You won't lay a hand on Nemera ever again."

Nemera blinked. She'd never heard this sort of possessiveness from Rowan. He was such a mild-tempered male. Where had this come from? Did she want to be his? Some part of her knew she should be afraid of him. He was a vampire—a creature designed to kill her kind. But the immortal who could easily rip out her throat was the only one who'd ever made her feel safe and wanted.

He wants me.

Unlike her husband, Rowan wanted *her*. Not just any woman. Not to have a wife for appearances or for the convenience of having another do all the domestic labor. He wanted *her*.

And she wanted him, too.

Somehow, in mere days, something had blossomed in her chest. It felt like she'd known him before, perhaps in another life. She didn't want to let that feeling go.

"Leave as the enchantress asked, and I'll go with you," Rowan said, his voice strangely calm. "I'll come to the next village or city and be in the auction. I won't fight you. But only if you leave at once."

Suddenly, a smile spread across Jonas' lips before he nodded. "You have yourself a deal."

Jonas stood and extended an arm toward Rowan.

Rising to his feet, Rowan went to him. Nemera watched in horror as Jonas slung an arm over Rowan's shoulders—as though they were old comrades—and ushered him toward a back hallway.

Something inside of Nemera fractured, nameless and screaming.

No. This couldn't be happening. She'd just gotten him back. After everything they'd done and gone through, they couldn't be back to where they started—with Rowan under Jonas' control.

"Come, my boy," Jonas said, his back to Nemera and Arabella. "There's much to prepare. We leave at sundown."

Finally finding her voice, Nemera said, "No! Rowan, you can't do this."

He glanced over his shoulder, his eyes full of... Was that regret?

"Please," she begged. "Don't do this."

This couldn't be the last time she'd see him.

With a final glance back, his blue eyes flickering between hers as though to encapsulate her in his mind, he turned and disappeared down a hallway.

As Jonas had promised, no one touched her. His guards turned and left, and then it was just her and Arabella in the common room—all the tables empty.

Fingers gripped Nemera's shoulder, pulling her out of her chair and out of the House of Obscurities.

"The two of you are hopeless," Arabella said, her voice full of exasperation as they strode across the street and down an alley. "I can't take you anywhere."

"He was just trying to save me," Nemera said, sounding like she'd swallowed sand.

Again, Arabella sighed, slowing to a stop once they were fully in a darkened alley. "At least Jonas is leaving town."

"We can't leave him to Jonas," Nemera said, hearing the desperation she felt fill her voice.

All she could do was hope like hell that Arabella didn't plan to extricate herself now that the Jonas problem had been taken care of. Would she care what happened to Rowan? Would she still want to help? She'd turned a blind eye before. Would she do so again now?

Nemera would fight. Just as before, she wouldn't leave Rowan to Jonas. But she was a mere human, and if she tried to rescue Rowan alone, her odds of success were abysmal.

"No, we can't." A smile crept over Arabella's lips as wicked as the demons she hunted down. "Now, we hunt."

Swallowing, Nemera followed the enchantress through the shadows—toward the outer wall.

Chapter Twelve

ROWAN

Somewhere in the distance, the hour tolled midnight as Jonas and the entire traveling troupe rolled out of the gates of Shadowbank, the guards pocketing bags of coin.

Apparently, Jonas had taken Arabella's words to heart and left in the night to avoid the enchantresses.

The bars of Rowan's cage rattled as the cart moved over the uneven ground of the dirt roads leading out of the village. He gritted his teeth as the silver chains rattled, pressing against his bare skin and singeing his flesh.

Unlike before, Jonas didn't dress him in trousers, boots, and a shirt while traveling. No, to punish Rowan's disobedience—and loss in value now that he was no longer a virgin—he wore only ripped trousers that went to his mid-thigh. No shoes and no shirt. The silver cuffs scorched the flesh at his neck, wrists, and ankles.

With his handcuffs secured to the bottom of the barred cage, there was nothing he could do as the chains attaching his collar to the cuffs at his wrists brushed against his chest and arms. He grunted, biting back the pain. It felt like his flesh was on fire.

At least, he couldn't feel the cool evening air as a vampire. He wouldn't shiver in the night. No, he'd *burn*. The ringleader would see to that.

Jonas rode atop a horse just ahead of Rowan's cage, eyes scanning the dark land around them. The half-moon and the stars in the night sky illuminated the dirt road. But all light stopped at the forest's edge—the home of the demons.

Forming a circle around the troupe were a massive ring of vampires—at least two dozen of them. Both vampires from the original troupe and villagers who'd recently been turned.

Jonas had his guards turn a number of the villagers into vampires. Many were against their will—shoving vampire blood down their throats and snapping their necks. The journey to Shadowbank had cost many vampires their lives, and the vampires who'd been slain by demons needed replacing. Others were likely turned at a price. But none had been selected for auction. Apparently, only he had that *privilege*.

With the new vampires, the troupe had increased in number significantly, but the dangers had grown worse with more and more demon sightings. Even the performers were armed with blades and crossbows.

She's safe, he thought, allowing himself to conjure the image in his mind's eye of his redheaded mortal with fire in her veins. He'd never forget her scent of strawberries and sunshine and the way she'd given him all of her body and her hopes for the future—just for a chance at freedom. His freedom. He'd never forget the times he'd touched her and buried his face inside her even as he longed for her with his entire being.

She was more than her blood.

Sharp despair filled his every breath as the troupe rolled away in a train of horse-drawn carts, people on horseback, and the vampires moving on silent feet. But it was worth it.

He had known love in this life.

It was something he'd never thought was possible for him. Not with his upbringing with his father or since he was sold to Jonas. The most he'd dared hope for was kind mortals who weren't cruel with his body or bite when he was purchased. But

Nemera had given him something precious that he'd never forget. She'd given him herself.

He loved her.

The realization struck him, stealing his breath away. He'd fallen madly in love with her in a matter of days.

And he had only one regret—he wished he'd told her.

More than that, he wished there'd been more time.

As they moved in silence, only the whickering of horses and the bouncing of the wheels of the carts echoing in the night, he clung to the memories. For a time, it distracted him from the pain of the silver cuffs against his skin. But as the hours drew on and the pain rose like the ocean's tide, images of Nemera grew blurry in his mind. Hisses of pain turned into grunts as his nails dug grooves into the wooden base of his cage.

A small form appeared beside his barred cage, her hood pulled up and a crossbow in her hands. Even in the darkness, even with the constant agony of the silver against his skin, Rowan knew who it was.

"You were supposed to escape this life," Elowyn whispered, her eyes locked on Jonas' back from where he rode on a horse ahead of them. "What are you doing back here?"

"I had to." Rowan sighed, thinking of the last moments he'd seen Nemera in the common room and the look of betrayal in her eyes. "He would have killed Nemera otherwise."

She simply nodded. "I'll do what I can, but there may not be much any of us can do. Jonas has barely left your side."

"Don't," Rowan said. "I appreciate your wanting to help, but don't. Enough people have been hurt on my account."

The acrobat looked at him then, lines between her brows. Without another word, she returned to her place beside the others. There had to be forty performers in the troupe now. Perhaps more.

Inhuman noises echoed along the horizon, and he found his eyes drawn to the line of trees, skating the forest's edge and waiting for the first demon attack. Because it wasn't a matter of *if* they'd come. It was a matter of when.

There was a crunch of heavy steps atop underbrush, and the entire troupe halted and turned toward the forest.

A sudden thought struck him.

Perhaps he wouldn't make it to the auction after all. Maybe the demons would end them all this very night.

Chapter Thirteen

NEMERA

Nemera rode behind Arabella, following the enchantress' horse around a bend in the wall as they watched the troupe move through the ward that was a few hundred feet beyond the wall and leave Shadowbank. The purple-blue ward rippled like a stone dropped in water before stilling, casting a faint glow on the stretch of flat grass on either side.

As Arabella had predicted, Jonas left late in the night.

The horse whickered beneath Nemera, agitated by the shadows of the forest. Arabella's steed had a similar temperament. None of the beasts were easy this close to the forest. And Nemera could only hold on to hope that the horses would be calm enough to help them flee with what came next.

Her heart clenched as she spotted a silhouetted form inside of a cart with a large cage. Even from far away, she knew who it was.

Jonas wanted to humiliate Rowan after everything that had happened.

And he's back in his chains.

Rage filled her chest. Rowan deserved better than this. She didn't care that he was a vampire or that he fed on humans. He deserved kindness and happiness. And damn her, she wanted to be the one to give it to him.

She was a mere human in a world of so many powerful creatures. But she had to do what she could to help.

"Our only hope is a surprise attack," Arabella said, her eyes fixed on the troupe. "We need to get in, free Rowan, and get out."

Nemera nodded.

Arabella had explained that she couldn't bring other enchantresses to help them, as her sisters in the Quarter—which was near the front gates—would sense a magic wielder moving outside the wall. There was a chance they'd sense Arabella even now. But the risk would be greater the more enchantresses there were.

The troupe grew smaller in the distance as they moved down the dirt road—a road that so few dared to travel on.

Then Arabella snapped her reins and rode into the night. Nemera did likewise, barely clinging to the saddle.

I'm going to die, Nemera thought as they rode toward the troupe.

Her head swam as her breaths came in shallow bursts. Never in her life had she been outside the wall or ward of Shadowbank. Outside of what she'd done for Rowan, the scariest thing she'd ever done was dare to start her life over after her husband left her life and heart in tatters.

Now, beyond the wall and the protection of the ward, her heart raced like the pounding of the horse's hooves. She gripped the reins in sweaty fists, willing herself to keep her seat in the saddle. But with each passing moment, her heartbeat quickened, and she struggled to breathe.

"Take deep breaths," Arabella said over her shoulder.

It was then that Nemera realized she was hyperventilating. Bursts of light popped up at the edges of her vision, and her chest rose and fell in rapid succession.

Arabella slowed her horse so that she rode beside Nemera.

"You're no use to Rowan if you're panicking. And you're going to upset the horses."

Arabella was right.

Nemera took in several slow, deep breaths, trying to steady her racing heart.

"Sorry," Nemera managed after a few more trembling intakes of the too-cool night air.

"You're brave, you know," Arabella said, eyeing the empty horizon—beyond which the troupe had disappeared over a bend in the road. "Few would venture beyond the ward, even for their loved ones."

"I don't feel brave," Nemera said, rubbing a fist into the center of her chest, trying to loosen the tightness there.

"There's no courage without fear," Arabella said. "Even I'm afraid. I'm good at what I do." She gestured to the two crossing blades on her back. "But I'm not defeat-twenty-vampires-single-handedly good."

"Don't tell me that," Nemera said, squeezing her eyes shut. "I need to pretend that at least one of us isn't about to shit our pants."

Arabella chuckled. "Let's get Rowan and get behind the ward before Jonas notices—or worse, before we attract the attention of demons. If demons do attack, we will have minutes to get behind the ward. When one comes, more will follow."

Bile rose in Nemera's throat.

I'm too small for all of this, she thought. *Too insignificant in this world of enchantresses and vampires and demons.*

But she gripped the reins and thought of Rowan in the cage on the wagon.

In silence, she followed Arabella on horseback as the enchantress rode toward the troupe. To her surprise, when they caught up with the troupe a few miles later, hiding behind a cluster of trees, the troupe had stopped and were setting up camp. Only the vampires didn't prepare for a night of rest. They kept their ring around the troupe, facing outwards.

Dismounting, Arabella ushered her horse deeper into the cluster of trees they hid behind, tying its reins loosely to a branch. Nemera did likewise.

"Stay here," Arabella said to her. "I'm going to take as many of the vampires out as I can who are guarding nearby, and then we'll sneak into camp together."

Nemera nodded, remaining by the horses.

She watched as Arabella moved her arms in sweeping motions, the wind seeming to harden as she did so before snapping out. There was a rustling in the grass before a vampire appeared, pulled into the cluster of trees—and out of sight of the troupe.

She didn't recognize the male, and she thought to wonder whether he was a villager she'd never met or someone who'd come with Jonas' troupe. The male struggled as Arabella trapped him with her magic, tying him down before freeing a long dagger from a sheath at her waist and plunging it into his chest. A silver dagger, she realized.

He clawed and scraped at Arabella's arm, and blood traveled from where his fingernails had broken her skin in dark rivulets.

Eventually, he stilled, and ever so slowly, his body dissolved into ash—turning from flesh and blood, once vibrant with life, to a crumbling husk.

Nemera covered her nose and mouth with the corner of her cloak as the ash was carried away on a faint breeze.

Arabella took down two more vampires in this way. One sunk his fangs into Arabella's neck before she could fell him with her silver blade. He, too, faded away on a dark breeze, his ashes disappearing as though he never even was.

Arabella muttered, "Fuck." She pressed her fingertips to the puncture wounds on her neck, where more blood was trailing down. It was faint, but was it enough to draw the attention of nearby demons?

Suddenly, the enchantress froze, her eyes growing distant.

"What is it?" Nemera whispered.

Arabella didn't respond. Instead, she remained utterly still, her gaze growing distant.

"Enchantress?"

Then there was a sound in the distance like the screeching of crows and tearing of realms.

Fear sliced through Nemera. For a long moment, she froze, her mind going utterly blank. A single tear slipped down her cheek. Another sound tore through the nearby forest, much closer this time. A wave of deep, unrelenting terror filled her chest like hot, sticky tar.

"Belgor," Arabella said as she ran for the horses, freeing their reins. She pushed the reins to Nemera's horse into her hands.

"It feeds on fear. We must have attracted its attention," Arabella said as she mounted her horse. "It might have smelled my blood. Or maybe it smelled the troupe's fear." When Nemera still stood where she was, Arabella said, "Get on, *now*. Or we're both dead."

Shaking herself, Nemera managed to get her foot into one stirrup and hoisted herself up.

Nemera's fear would be the equivalent of a beacon to this demon. It would be drawn to her like a moth to a flame. Only, this moth would snuff out her light if it caught up with them.

Something cracked behind them. It sounded like the snapping of trees, like the severing of trunks.

How big was the belgor? Was it so big, so strong, that it could fell trees in a feeding frenzy?

With a snap of her reins, Arabella galloped forward—toward the troupe. Nemera hurried after her. They had to save Rowan. It was now or never.

A dark shape emerged from the forest.

"Don't look back," Arabella called over her shoulder.

Swallowing the bile back, Nemera did as she was told, keeping her eyes ahead as they galloped. Ahead of them, there was screaming in the camp. Small tents were knocked over, trampled as dozens of the performers hurried to grab crossbows and aim them outward—toward Arabella, Nemera, and the belgor. The remaining vampires were moving, a mere blur as they ran to form a line between the troupe and the oncoming demon.

The thing behind them roared, and it sounded like the fracturing of the core of the earth.

It must be mere yards behind them now.

But as the horses leaped over the twisting roots of trees—only paces from the line of vampires—Nemera spotted movement.

Then everything happened at once.

In one moment, Nemera was atop her horse, leaning low and clutching the reins. In the next moment, there was a snapping of the wind and something like a band of energy wrapped around her waist. She flew off her horse and into the air. As her arms pinwheeled, she watched in slow motion as Arabella moved her arms in sweeping motions, pulling Nemera in an arc above her with her magic.

Nemera managed a glance behind her and spotted a creature of nightmares as it leaped at her horse—where she'd just been.

The belgor was a creature of flesh and shadow. It had two massive, twisting horns atop its head that was as dark as the rest of its body. A cluster of small skulls on its shoulder wailed like the fracturing of human hope. It was easily three or four times the size of the tallest human she'd ever seen. At the end of its hands and feet, there were talons as long as her head. But what drew her eyes the most was its two eyeless sockets that seemed to drain the light from the night sky.

It ignored her horse, leaping over it and landing on all fours before rising on two legs.

Nemera hovered in the air for a moment longer before she crashed into the grass and tumbled. The world spun as she rolled again and again, stones scraping against exposed skin. Eventually, the spinning stopped, and she fumbled as she struggled to her feet. Everything in her screamed to lie down, to freeze and hope the demon would lose interest in her. But if she was about to die, it wouldn't be lying down.

As her vision stilled, she spotted Arabella, who continued to move her arms in a swirling motion from where she was on horseback. The belgor charged her, but it ran into what seemed to be an invisible wall and screeched. As it did, the horses from the troupe neighed, and humans screamed.

The demon turned from the enchantress, its eyeless gaze settling on the troupe. Then it was moving—toward the performers and the line of vampires surrounding them.

For reasons Nemera didn't understand, the creature had decided that a line of vampires was less threatening than one enchantress.

Arabella dismounted and was running toward her. Looping an arm under Nemera's, the enchantress hauled her to her feet.

"Sorry about that," Arabella said, her breaths even.

Nemera waved a trembling hand. "Nothing to be sorry about. You saved my life. I'll gladly take temporary flight over the belgor getting me."

In unison, their gazes turned toward where the demon fought against the vampires. The vampires were clearly untrained as they moved in haphazard pairings or individually, attacking the demon at random. It batted them away, sending vampires flying dozens of feet away. Even without training, they maintained the line between the demon and the performers.

"Rowan." The word sounded like a prayer on Nemera's lips. "I have to protect him. He'll be helpless against this demon in his silver shackles."

Arabella pressed a blade into her hand. "Go. I'll stay here to help the vampires."

Turning, Nemera's gaze settling on Jonas where he sat atop his horse—safely behind the line of vampires. He had a sword in one hand and the other held on to his reins. His eyes were fixed on Nemera, full of hatred. She narrowed her eyes in return, allowing her anger to seep into every pore, every fiber of her being.

Just how many of these vampires did Jonas turn against their will like Rowan? Had any of them consented to this life?

She turned back to the belgor—where it attempted to feed on a vampire, only to be pulled off its prey and shoved backward by another vampire. This happened again and again as at least twenty vampires closed in on the demon.

Distantly, she registered Arabella joining the fight. She'd placed herself between the human performers and the demon, blocking it from advancing. For that reason and many others, Nemera found herself admiring the female. She was far braver than Nemera could ever be. But Nemera clutched the remains of her courage and turned from the battle with the belgor.

Then she was running toward the troupe.

Some vampires turned toward her, their noses in the air as they sniffed, and she thought she saw their pupils swell in their eyes. But the moment they turned away from the belgor, it leaped on them. It knocked the vampires onto their backs and pulled something from them—a black, shimmering cloud rippling from the vampire's entire being and narrowing into a single stream. The belgor sucked it into its mouth, and she thought she saw little wisps flow into the screaming skulls on the demon's shoulder.

It's feeding on the vampire's fear, she realized.

The moment it finished feeding, the vampire's body evaporated into a plume of dust.

Nemera clapped a hand over her mouth, nearly retching, but stumbled toward the caravan that was now in chaos. To her relief, neither the performers with crossbows nor the vampires moved to stop her. Even Jonas had disappeared.

As she ran into the encampment, horses whinnied, kicking up and pulling against reins as humans tried to calm them. Performers ran in every direction with bundles in their arms, screaming. Some were in their sleeping garments and were fumbling to pull on boots or cloaks. One wagon was overturned, baskets of food rolling into the grass.

In the chaos, she struggled to locate Rowan's wagon with the cage.

She moved around carriages, weaving around screaming

humans—feeling tempted to join them and succumb to panic. Just when she feared Jonas had taken Rowan and fled the troupe, her eyes settled on the wagon with the cage. Only, instead of seeing Rowan's silhouetted figure inside, the door to the cage was open.

Without willing them, her feet were moving, and she was running toward the cage.

"Rowan!" she screamed, a terror deeper than anything she felt for the belgor filling her.

Had the demon already gotten to him? But his shackles weren't there. Wouldn't the chains remain if the belgor had fed on him? The other vampires had turned into a plume of dust. She clung to the shred of hope that he might still be alive somewhere —though helpless with the silver draining his strength. She had to find him.

For a moment, she stared at the empty cage, clinging to the blade Arabella had given her and shaking her head. Where could he be?

Turning on a heel, her eyes fell on a sight that had her freezing in place.

Jonas stood behind Rowan, a hand wrapped around the vampire's neck, pressing the silver collar into his skin. In his other hand, he held a knife over his heart. Rowan wore only torn trousers that came above his knee. The ringleader's hardened gaze locked on her as though he'd been expecting her. As though he'd known she'd come.

Instinctively, she raised her hands, but she didn't drop the knife.

"Don't hurt him," Nemera said. "Let him go."

"This is all your doing," Jonas hissed as though she hadn't spoken. "I assume you and that bitch enchantress brought the belgor on us."

"We didn't mean to," Nemera said, a faint tremble in her voice. "We were just trying to get Rowan back."

Jonas' fingers tightened, pulling Rowan's head back toward him—baring his throat further.

Even from where she stood yards away, she could smell the scent of roasting flesh—Rowan's skin burning against the silver cuffs and chains. Her eyes watered, and she blinked back the tears.

Rowan's eyes found hers. There was fear there, genuine fear, but there was also relief. His eyes skittered down to the blade in her hand.

Brows drawing together, an idea started to form in her mind.

"You've been so much trouble," Jonas said over the screaming performers, many of whom had joined the line of archers with crossbows near to the fighting vampires. "Deal or not, you'll die tonight, little bitch, for all you've done."

"The vampires," she said, swallowing. "Did they consent to being turned?"

A smile crept over Jonas' lips like the cracking of glaciers as it swept across his features. "What does it matter?"

"If I'm going to die, I'd like to know," she said. "Call it a dying wish."

As she spoke, she dared a slow step forward.

"No," Jonas said. "At least, not most of them."

"Why aren't they in cages?" she asked. "Are none of them going to be auctioned?"

He raised a brow, allowing his gaze to settle on Rowan once more. Slowly, as though caressing a lover, he ran the blade over Rowan's chest. The touch was light enough that it didn't break skin. He swirled the knife over Rowan's nipple, and Rowan hissed. It was then she realized what the blade was.

Silver.

Like the cuffs and the chains.

"Too old," Jonas said, his voice indifferent. "No virgins. Nothing particularly marketable. These are good for exactly what they're doing."

"Protecting your ass," she said, gesturing to where the

vampires held back the belgor. At least six had fallen, but there had to be about twenty remaining. Beside them, Arabella unleashed her magic on the demon.

One of Jonas' nostrils twitched upward.

Slowly, Nemera lowered her hands, daring another step forward.

"Don't move," the ringleader hissed, pressing the tip of the blade half an inch into Rowan's chest above his heart. "Take another step, and your lover boy is dead."

Rowan grunted but didn't move.

Nemera continued to walk forward. "Did you know new vampires can't control their thirst? Not when they're so recently turned."

Jonas' frown deepened. "And?"

"And," Nemera continued. "I wonder just how much any vampire can control themselves at the smell of blood—a lot of blood."

Then she raised the knife in her hand, drawing it down from the top of her forearm to her wrist. Pain sliced through her, hot and wet, but she didn't hold back. She pressed deeply enough that blood streamed down her arm, plopping heavily into the grass beneath her feet. Quickly, she ran the knife down her opposite arm, feeling the sharp kiss of the blade. As blood flowed down both arms, she found that standing became a little more difficult. But she locked her knees and bit back the pain.

As she'd hoped, Rowan's fangs emerged, and his pupils swelled. The concern in his gaze faded as his eyes settled on the blood dripping down her arms. The male she'd fallen for had disappeared and was replaced by the predator.

He'd shown her more care in days than her husband had in years. Through him, she'd learned what it was like to feel someone want the best for her and what true emotional safety was like. The gentle touches, his desire for her to know pleasure as well, his wanting to protect her from Jonas and his guards... All the moments they'd spent together swirled through her mind at once before settling on one simple truth.

"It's going to be okay," she said before she made a long slice across her collarbone. She hissed at the pain, but she didn't stop until wet, sticky warmth soaked through her shirt. Soon, dizziness settled over her vision.

She was losing too much blood too quickly.

Rowan pulled against Jonas' grip, his chains rattling. His pupils were entirely dilated now, and his lips peeled back to reveal massive canines. Eyes fixed on her, he tried to launch himself forward, but Jonas clung to him, barely holding him back.

It was then Nemera thought to wonder whether new vampires were stronger, too, and didn't just have the most alluring bite.

Sweat beaded Jonas' forehead as he tried to hold on to Rowan, but he couldn't keep the blade over his heart. Not as the vampire spun.

In a motion too fast for her eyes to track, Rowan wrapped the chains around Jonas' neck. Fisting the chains in either hand, he pulled. Jonas' eyes widened as though, in that moment, he realized death had come for him. That after all this time of dolling out death and immortality to others, all this time of selling people like they were mere objects without dreams or wishes, that his time had finally come to an end. The ringleader gripped the silver chains that he had used to control Rowan in either fist. Nemera watched as trails of smoke swiveled into the air as his immortal flesh roasted from the touch of silver. He pulled against the chains, trying to loosen Rowan's grip, but it was no use.

Snarling, Rowan pulled on the chains, the skin on his own palms a bright scarlet. Then there was a distinct *crack* as the ringleader's neck snapped.

The ringleader was dead.

There was another flash of movement as Rowan grabbed a key from Jonas' body and unlocked his shackles, tossing them to the ground in a hiss.

As he turned toward her, his eyes were void of recognition—a fathomless abyss that knew only hunger.

She didn't bother to run. She wouldn't make it far, anyway. This had been her doing. She'd instigated the beast within him to come forth. If there was any hope of defeating Jonas, it was if Rowan lost himself to the vampire—if he was too incensed by the scent of blood for his shackles to restrain him. She couldn't let him hold back, not on her account. Because somehow, she knew that he'd never give in to the vampire within. Not if it meant she'd be in danger.

There was a flash of movement to her right.

Before she could turn toward it, there was a second flash as Rowan appeared beside her, ripping the head of a vampire from its shoulders. A vampire that had been about to feed on her.

She'd forgotten that the scent of her blood would draw other vampires.

Even a few hundred feet from the battle with the belgor— where the vampires were now surrounding it and bringing it down—the smell of her blood could have some vampires leaving the demon to *feed*.

Suddenly, it was too much to stand. Exhaustion settled over her limbs, and her eyes fluttered closed as she fell toward the ground. Before she could, arms wrapped around her, keeping her from crashing into the earth.

It was in that moment that she realized the way Rowan held her, his fangs angled above her neck, it was just like how they'd met in the House of Obscurities in the basement on the round stage. The same stage she'd been auctioned on, and he'd rescued her from. Only this time, instead of leaning into her with slow care, he descended upon her.

His tongue ran over her collarbone where she'd cut herself before, and he licked her chest clean of blood. He moaned as though tasting the finest delicacy before lapping the blood on her arms.

Reaching up, she interlaced her fingers into his dark hair, marveling at the softness of it.

He'd never forgive her for this. She worried he'd never forgive himself. But she clung to the knowledge that, at long last, he'd be free.

Then the vampire sunk his fangs into her neck.

When he pulled her blood into his mouth, it wasn't slow or gentle. Instead, the lightheadedness she felt increased tenfold. As he drank, desire filled her, swelling in her chest and between her legs. She whimpered, unable to do more than succumb to the waves of pleasure rolling over her. As he took draft after draft of her blood into his mouth, her strength waned. She couldn't fight him even if she wanted to, and the desire swelling through her had her relaxing into his touch further. He was so much stronger, and she was so tired.

This wasn't Rowan though. She'd summoned the blood-sucking beast, and she'd known there was no coming back from this. He'd feed on her until his thirst was sated, and it wouldn't be anytime soon.

She watched through drooping eyelids how the reddened skin around his wrists softened to a pink that was far closer to the paleness of his skin.

As her eyes fluttered closed, she heard Arabella's voice.

"Rowan."

The enchantress' tone was like the snapping of a whip.

To Nemera's surprise, the pull of blood through her veins stopped, and she felt him remove his lips from her neck. She gasped as his fangs pulled free of her skin, but she didn't have the energy to pick up her head from where it dangled in his arms. She didn't even have the energy to open her eyes.

Instead, she felt herself drifting from consciousness, and she knew it was for the last time.

"It's okay," she tried to say, but her lips never moved.

Don't hurt him, she thought toward Arabella.

But there was nothing more she could do. Not as she faded from this world—in the arms of a vampire.

Chapter Fourteen

ROWAN

"The battle is over now. Put her down," a female hissed somewhere beyond his line of sight. "The belgor is dead. Jonas is dead."

Taking one last swallow, he removed his lips from the neck of his prey.

Who *dared* to interrupt him? He would unleash himself upon whoever had tried to keep him from his feast.

Slowly, he released his prey, which tumbled to the ground in a lifeless heap. Not bothering to see where it landed, he narrowed his gaze upon his next prey.

This one was female as well. His heightened senses detected she wasn't like the female he'd just devoured. This one was powerful, and she held two blades before her—one sword and one knife. Only one was silver. But no matter. They would be little more than a nuisance.

"Step away," the female said, her weapons raised in his direction as she remained in a lowered crouch. "You won't touch her again."

He hissed, showing his fangs to the female.

She wore all black as though she were night incarnate, her

hood pushed back. Only her pale skin and the gemstone between her brows reflected the light of the moon. And her blades.

Who was she to tell him what to do?

"You've just killed the woman who risked everything to save you," the female said as she stepped toward him. "It was her idea to use her blood to free you from Jonas. Without her quick thinking, you might be dead."

Something in her words had him pausing.

Frowning, his thoughts moved of their own accord, hanging on the name "Jonas." Why did that name stir recognition within him? Why did fury fill his veins as much as the blood from his most recent prey? He was the predator. No one and nothing should make him feel this way.

But he sensed the female continuing to step toward him. Again, he hissed, and she paused, freezing in place where she stood several yards away.

He stepped forward, prepared to take down this female once and for all. But as he did, his foot brushed against something. For reasons he couldn't explain, he looked down. His eyes fell upon a female with curly hair as bright as the blood he yearned for.

"Nemera," said the female with the blades, though her voice was distant to his ears. "Her name is Nemera."

He blinked at the weak human beneath his boot. She lay on her side, her body limp and her arms splayed. Red curls fell across her forehead and spread in the grass all around her like a fiery crown.

She was so pale. It was as though her skin was translucent. There were long cuts down both arms and a cut across her chest just beneath her collarbone.

Why would a human do something so foolish? Surely, she knew that bleeding near so many vampires would result in her demise.

It was her idea to use her blood to free you from Jonas.
The warrior's words came back to him.
Had this female died on purpose? For him?

"Nemera."

His lips formed the name, unbidden.

A single image glanced across his mind—holding this small woman in his arms in an alley with the smell of the ocean breeze and her desire lingering in the air.

Freedom.

Home.

He knew in that instant there was something he yearned for more than blood.

The hunger receded, and Rowan gasped as memories flooded back to him.

"Nemera!" he screamed as he fell to his knees before her too-still body.

"Oh, no." He ran cool fingers over her cheeks, which had lost their usual warmth. "What have I done?"

Something cracked inside of him. A bellow emerged from the depths of his shattered heart—from his being where he'd learned not to hope, not to long for anything more than what he'd been given in this life. But he'd *yearned* for this woman. He wanted her. He wanted a life with her and everything that entailed. The world was leached of color without her bright radiance, and he didn't want to remain in it without her.

The enchantress kneeled beside him.

Arabella reached out and pressed her fingers to Nemera's throat. She started and glanced over to him. "She's not dead. Not yet. But she doesn't have long."

Something like hope swelled in his chest.

"Help her," he said, his voice cracking. "I beg you. I'll do anything."

As Arabella shook her head, his remaining hope disintegrated, and tears fell down his cheeks.

I've killed her, he thought as he pulled Nemera's limp body into his arms. *I'm going to lose her, and it's all my fault.*

He held her to his chest, listening with his heightened senses for her heartbeat. After a moment, he heard it, but it was so faint.

It was nearly indistinct, even to his senses. He held her tighter, feeling her curls tickle his cheeks and nose.

So much life. There had been so much life in her. And he'd stripped that from her.

Disgust filled his chest, but he didn't let her go. His tears fell into her hair, and he breathed in her scent of strawberries and sunshine. He wished he could hold her and breathe her in for the rest of his existence.

"One of the other enchantresses with healing magic might be able to heal her, but I can't. My magic isn't strong in healing," Arabella said. "But you could heal her."

His head snapped up.

"How?"

The enchantress opened and closed her fists, pressing them to her thighs where she knelt.

"Vampires are renowned for the pleasure from their bites, but their blood—your blood—is even more precious," she said. "I read in an old text that it has a magical property. If you give it to a human who's injured, it *should* heal them."

He frowned. "Vampire blood turns mortals into blood-sucking monsters if they die with it in their system. If it doesn't heal her in time, she'd become a vampire. I couldn't do that to her —make her a vampire without her consent. Not after what Jonas did to me."

The enchantress licked her lips before she said, "It's a risk. If it doesn't heal her in time, if we're too late, she'll become a vampire. Are you willing to lose her? Because if you don't try right now, then she will die."

Words failed him, and he shook his head. "I can't without her consent. That would make me no better than Jonas."

"Taking someone's choice from them—when they have a voice to say what they want—is evil," Arabella said. "But Nemera can't choose right now. She needs you to choose for her. She needs you to fight for her."

Tears flowed down his cheeks and into Nemera's hair as he

held her close. Her heartbeat slowed further, growing even fainter. He had mere moments to decide, or she'd be gone forever.

The thought that this woman—who was as kind as she was brave—had risked everything to save him had something blossoming inside of his chest. Someone had fought for him. Someone had thought he was precious, something worth saving. In that moment, he wanted nothing more than to tell her he loved her. He wanted to give her the world.

But first, he had to risk taking the world from her.

"I'll do it."

As gently as he could, he lowered Nemera to the ground and wiped the tears from his cheeks with the back of a hand.

Arabella offered him a knife, which he took. He ran the blade over his palm and pressed the bleeding cut to Nemera's lips.

Come back to me.

He watched as rivulets of his blood streamed down either side of her face as she remained there, unmoving.

"Drink! Drink, Nemera, please!" he cried.

But she didn't move.

Arabella shifted so that she was across from him over Nemera's body and began moving her arms in sweeping motions. "Keep trying. I'll use what little healing magic I have. Hopefully, between the two of us, we can bring her back. But she *must* ingest your blood, or all is lost."

He thought of the times he'd fed on Nemera and how he'd pulled her blood into his mouth when he fed. An idea struck, and he pressed his palm to his lips before sucking blood into his mouth. Once he had a mouthful, he leaned down so his lips were above Nemera's. Droplets of blood lingered on her lips and cheeks.

They'd never kissed. Not properly. They'd shared many other things, but they hadn't shared this. And he hated the idea of their only kiss being shared in this way. He wanted to do it properly. But in that moment, he knew that this might be the only way he could get her to drink his blood.

So, he lowered his lips and pressed them to hers.

They were as soft as he'd dreamed.

But he didn't let himself linger. Slowly, he released the blood into Nemera's mouth from his, letting it trickle in. As he did, he pinched her nose shut with a hand.

For a long moment, nothing happened.

He could no longer hear her heartbeat, and he couldn't feel the rise and fall of her chest. The only thing he could hear was the shift of Arabella's leathers as she used her magic beside him. But he continued to trickle his blood into Nemera's mouth, praying this wouldn't be the last time he kissed her. The last time he held her alive.

Suddenly, Nemera's body shifted. He pulled back, watching with wide eyes as Nemera coughed. He helped her lean onto her side as she gasped and spat out blood. When she had finished and turned back to him, no fangs protruded from her lips.

Relief flooded his chest, his entire being.

Nemera was alive. The woman he loved was alive.

Hesitantly, he reached out and traced a finger over her skin where her shirt had torn open from where she'd cut herself down the length of her arm. The cut was gone. The skin was completely healed. More importantly, her skin was warm.

She wasn't a vampire.

They'd saved her before she'd died with vampire blood in her system. He breathed a sigh of relief. He hadn't taken her choice from her. And he hadn't lost her forever.

Tears streamed down his cheeks, and he realized suddenly that tears were falling down hers as well. Distantly, he registered Arabella standing and striding away. He also registered that he could no longer hear the roars of the belgor. Outside of the sounds of horses and humans, the night was unusually quiet this close to the forest.

Except for the sound of Nemera's heartbeat.

He'd never heard something so beautiful before.

"Do it again," Nemera said, not bothering to brush her tears away, which mingled with blood on her face.

Brows furrowing, he said, "Do what?"

"Kiss me," she said, brushing her hair back. "Please."

A smile as bright and warm as the dawn spread across his face.

"I'll kiss you every day until the sun stops rising in the sky," Rowan said. "And even then, I won't stop kissing you."

She reached out, running a thumb over his cheek. Then she leaned forward and pressed a kiss to one cheek and then the next, kissing his tears away.

The feel of her lips on his skin had something inside of him melded back together, and he wondered if it was the fractured pieces of his heart or his hope for this life. Because he wanted to enjoy every moment, every breath with her. Suddenly, everything in the world felt right, as though this was exactly where he was meant to be—with her.

Then he kissed her, fusing his lips with hers and pulling her close. He marveled at the feel of her warmth, the life in her veins. She was alive and his. And he was hers.

And it was perhaps the best moment of his life.

WHAT FELT LIKE MOMENTS LATER, Arabella appeared before them.

"We have to go," she said with an urgency in her tone. "Right fucking now."

In an instant, Rowan was on his feet, sweeping Nemera into his arms. "What is it?"

"The belgor is dead, but the battle attracted other demons," Arabella said. "We have to get back to Shadowbank. Now. Or we're all dead."

Arabella nodded to the remaining members of the troupe—performers, mostly—who were pulling horses free of carriages and mounting them bareback. He counted approximately thirty humans and twenty vampires. Bodies were strewn along the ground, some of which were in pieces—arms and legs scattered yards away from their bodies. Any vampires that had been felled by the belgor would have turned to ash on the wind.

"Anyone who wants to come to the village is welcome," the enchantress said, raising her voice to be heard above the rising voices around them. "The weak and wounded go on horseback."

Rowan watched as Elowyn limped over to a horse, a gash in her thigh. A performer hoisted her onto the back of a black mare.

Arabella turned on a heel and strode toward the back of the troupe. "Leave everything behind. If you try to bring your belongings with you, they will slow you down, and you *will* die. All remaining vampires, you're with me. We're bringing up the rear." She nodded to Rowan. As her eyes settled on Nemera, a relieved look crossed her features. "Not you, Rowan. Get her home safe."

He nodded.

He didn't have to be told twice.

From this day forward, Nemera was—and would always be—his priority.

Then they were all fleeing the plains, moving around wagons and stepping over the fallen. Some performers ran while others rode on horseback.

Slowing his pace to match the humans and their horses, he lingered for a moment. Even as the darkened plains raced by, the shadows in the forest grew. His ears picked up a deep, rattling sound. It was like the clacking of bones in the wind. As the moments ticked by, the clacking sounds increased in quantity until it sounded like a chorus of death.

Whatever was coming for them, it wasn't alone.

And the troupe was far too slow.

At this pace, it would take thirty minutes, maybe more, for the humans to get back to Shadowbank. Whatever came for them...

Well, it wouldn't be long now.

Picking up his pace, he moved with supernatural speed

toward the front of the group. Nemera—his small, beautiful, brave human—wrapped her arms around his neck, holding him close but said nothing.

A few moments later, Arabella shouted from behind them, where she ushered the performers on foot to move faster.

"The soulless!"

That explained the rattling sound.

Even he knew of the creatures of bones that fed on humans. The soulless were believed to have once been humans whose souls had been taken by one of the zaol, a greater demon. After, the once-humans were left as literal shells of themselves—creatures of bones that roamed the lands in search of the souls that were lost to them. Eating any living creature they came across hoping to reclaim a soul they would never again find.

They were the walking dead that couldn't be killed.

And they traveled in packs.

"Help the others," Nemera said, her voice trembling faintly.

As he raced across the open plains, he glanced down to the woman who had his heart—the woman who even now thought of others.

"Not until you're safe."

Then he sped ahead of the troupe of humans racing back toward safety. The land had started to shift from the full darkness of night, and a dark blue hovered over the land. As he moved, each blade of grass grew in visibility, and the shadows of the trees slowly receded back into the forest. But the soulless would be upon them before the sun shone on the land. It wouldn't deter or slow them.

Soon, the purple-blue dome of Shadowbank's ward came into view. It glowed and shimmered faintly like sunshine through stained glass.

He raced toward it, holding tightly to Nemera all the while.

He savored the feel of her warmth in his arms, how *real* she felt. She was everything he didn't know he needed.

Stopping before the billowing ward, he placed Nemera gently onto the ground.

Since he wasn't a demon, he could pass through the ward. It had been specifically designed to keep out demons of the forest—not vampires or shifters. But doing so exhausted him, as though the ward sensed he wasn't entirely mortal and fought against his entry. He needed to save all his strength for the fight ahead.

But did he want to fight?

Everything he wanted was right here. Nemera had been the only person to fight for him, to risk everything for him. And he'd nearly lost her because of it. Did he owe the humans of the troupe anything, especially after they'd remained idle in the months he'd been Jonas' captive? He thought of Elowyn and what she'd done to help him after he'd bought Nemera in the auction, and he thought of the fear he'd seen in the eyes of the performers when the belgor had descended upon them. He'd feared like them once. He'd felt vulnerable to the world, as though life was happening to him.

He'd wanted someone to fight for him. And someone had.

He couldn't leave them to die, not when there was something he could do about it. Even though everything inside of him yearned to scoop Nemera back into his arms and run through the ward and to safety, he knew he couldn't turn his back on the others.

Still, he hesitated, his brows drawing together as he looked over Nemera's too-pale face and skin. She'd lost too much blood.

"Can you make it through on your own?" he asked, reaching for her.

She waved him away. "I'll be fine. Go help the others."

Nodding, he started to leave and then paused. Turning back on a heel, he wrapped an arm around her lower back and pulled her into him.

His lips glanced against hers, moving until he felt her tongue flick against his. She tasted of sunshine and the hope of tomorrow. Too soon, he pulled away and released her slowly.

"Rowan, in case I don't get to tell you later, I—" she began, but he stopped her.

"Don't," he said. "Whatever it is, tell me when I'm back. When we're both safely behind this ward and we have all the time in the world. Tell me then. Okay?"

With a nod, she said, "Of course. Be careful."

Then she took a step back into the ward. It rippled for a moment before she was through.

Not letting himself look back at her a moment longer—or else he'd never leave—he turned and ran for the horizon, down the long dirt roads and toward the troupe.

As he ran, the rattle of bones sounded in the line of trees, followed by a wordless screech.

They'd officially run out of time.

Chapter Fifteen

NEMERA

Nemera paced in the grass at the edge of the ward.

There was a few hundred feet of an open grassy plain between the wall and the ward. On the other side of the ward, the grass continued for half a mile, sloping uphill to the dark forest. To her left, there were a few miles of grass, beyond which were the fields and beyond that was the bay. To the right, the dirt road stretched on for countless miles back toward civilization.

Behind her, guards shouted, telling her to get behind the wall. But she ignored them. It was bad enough she wasn't able to help the others and had to hide behind the ward. She wouldn't hide behind the wall as well. In case anyone needed help when they stumbled through the barrier, she was going to be there.

She didn't know what she'd be able to do to help in her current state, but she had to try.

I almost died, she thought as her limbs trembled so badly that she had to stop pacing. Her body screamed at her to sit, to *rest,* but she locked her knees and forced herself to remain standing.

She hadn't died. Somehow, Rowan and Arabella had brought her back. They'd have a lot to talk about when all of this was over.

She stared at the horizon where the dirt road turned and disappeared beyond view.

There were countless miles of open land between Shadowbank and the next human settlement. And because Shadowbank was so remote, they had only the uneven dirt roads that forged a path into the wild lands next to the forest that was the home of the demons.

With so many of Jonas' vampires dead, the remaining humans of the troupe were vulnerable. But she couldn't think on that too hard. They were going to make it. Somehow, they would all make it back. She instead tried to focus on the relief she felt now that Rowan was free of Jonas. The world was free of Jonas.

When the horizon remained empty for long minutes, she feared the soulless had overtaken the troupe.

Come on, she thought. *Come on.*

Her heart raced so fast that her vision blurred. The idea of living without Rowan—something she'd had to consider far too many times recently—had something inside of her chest caving in. She'd only known him for days, and yet he'd become a part of what she dreamed of for the future. He'd gone from being a stranger to someone she craved to be near. She longed not just for him to be free of his chains but to see him smile—to see him smile at *her*. The time they'd shared, while beautiful, wasn't near enough. She wanted more time with him to explore the depths of his heart, his very being, and interlace her hopes with his.

He'd shown her kindness, more care than she'd ever experienced before. And she didn't want to let him go.

She knew she'd had something she needed to tell him before. She hadn't yet known what it was. But in that moment, she knew what her heart had been trying to say.

I love him, she realized. *I love a vampire.*

She looked back to the road.

They had to make it. They just had to.

Suddenly, there was movement on the horizon a few miles

out, like the shimmering heat above a road on a hot summer's day.

She breathed a sigh of relief. But her relief didn't last long.

The troupe emerged above the nearby hill, crossing the horizon and speeding toward the ward. Those on horseback came first, riding like mad. Farther behind, humans raced on foot, staggering forward, some falling onto knees and being heaved upright and shoved forward.

There was a blur of movement, and then Rowan was before her with a girl in his arms. She couldn't be more than twelve.

Tears filled the girl's eyes as Rowan placed her down, and she looked around. Then she paused, her eyes lingering on the translucent purple-blue ward, as though it was the single thing anchoring her in this world. For long moments, she didn't move, and Nemera worried the girl might succumb to shock.

"This way," Nemera said, gesturing her forward. "Quickly."

The girl took a step forward, stumbled, caught herself, and then hurried through the ward.

Somehow, Nemera managed to catch her and remain upright even though her body felt like a leaf waving in the wind. The girl was dressed in what looked like an acrobat's costume. Burying her face in Nemera's chest, tears spilled down her cheeks. Nemera ran a hand over the girl's hair, making shushing sounds. All the while, her eyes were fixed on the too-slow troupe.

Behind them, shadowy figures emerged.

They flooded out of the forest like a dark current. Some figures climbed over others, clawing their way forward on all fours. There were dozens of them. No, hundreds. More and more skeletal figures came into view, running from the forest behind the humans.

Rowan appeared again, depositing a middle-aged woman with what appeared to be a broken leg. Like the girl, he placed her on the ground outside of the ward before disappearing in a blur.

As the woman hurried through the ward, the girl in Nemera's arms rushed for her. But Nemera didn't have eyes for them.

Instead, her gaze fixed on the line of vampires and the single enchantress holding back the horde of soulless.

Now that they were closer, she could see them more clearly.

They were the skeletal remains of humans. A shadowy sinew seemed to hold the bones together, wisps of darkness flowing off their bodies. She thought she heard a hissing sound above the sound of rattling of bones that permeated through her very being.

But as she watched Arabella move her arms in sweeping motions and the air respond in kind, sending the soulless flying backwards, she knew one fact with utter clarity.

They wouldn't make it to the ward in time.

Nemera turned and was running for the wall. Her body gave out, and she staggered to a knee. Her vision spun, and the earth beneath her seemed to tilt. But she picked out the wall and the main gate, forced herself back to her feet, and managed a limping-gait toward it.

"They need help!" Nemera shouted when she was at the base of the multiple-story stone wall beside the gate. "Send enchantresses! Enchantress Arabella is out there."

Arabella had risked her life to save Rowan, and now, she needed rescuing.

Nemera might not have magic, but this was something she could do—asking for help.

The gate rumbled before it opened.

Dozens of guards ran across the top of the wall with bows in hand. Others held crossbows and moved toward openings before aiming arrows outward—toward the oncoming horde. Did they think the demons could get through? But that was impossible.

"Come inside!" guards shouted to her and the other performers who'd made it through the ward, but Nemera shook her head.

"Enchantress Jessamine," she insisted, recalling the enchantress who had been at Arabella's side when she and Rowan had asked for help. "Please go find her."

She thought she saw guards disappear from the wall, but there was so much movement of bodies and shouting as archers prepared their formations and soldiers ran with swords along the top of the wall. Where were the enchantresses? She didn't spot any black leather.

Sighing, she turned back toward the ward.

Rowan had brought back a few more performers, but there were far too few. At least fifteen humans were running, nearly overcome by the soulless. But those on horseback rode through the ward, which separated for them as they hurtled forward.

A hand was on her shoulder, squeezing.

Nemera turned back, eyes widening. An enchantress dressed in black leather from head to toe stood beside her, a sword in one hand. Her long blonde hair was tied back, and Nemera could tell in the way her wide hips leaned to one side that exasperation filled her to her very core.

Relief flooded Nemera's chest. "Enchantress Jessamine!" She pointed toward where Arabella and the vampires were fighting to hold back the line of demons—and losing. "Arabella is out there. She needs help—"

"I knew that bitch was going to do something heroic," Jessamine hissed. "She should've asked for backup."

"She was worried it would draw too much attention," Nemera said, blinking back the surprise at hearing Arabella spoken about with anything but the utmost respect.

The enchantress released Nemera's shoulder.

"Of course she was." Jessamine pinched the bridge of her nose.

Two more enchantresses appeared at Jessamine's side.

Unlike Jessamine, who was short even by human standards, these two enchantresses were taller. One was thickly muscled and built like a tree, and the second had blonde hair like Jessamine, but it came to her shoulders. Her eyes held a kindness that had Nemera wondering if she would fare well in battle.

"Brynne, Cora," Jessamine said without looking at them. "Took you long enough." She gestured to where Arabella fought alongside the vampires. They were maybe a mile outside of the ward now.

"Let's go," Jessamine said, and then she was running.

As they plunged through the ward—and toward the horde of the undead—dozens of enchantresses appeared on either side of Nemera, dashing toward the ward where more humans were fleeing inside. They ran past her until they formed a line at the edge of the ward, just inside of it. By the movements of their arms, Nemera could tell that they were using magic, though she didn't know what they were doing.

But Jessamine, Brynne, and Cora threw themselves through the ward and ran into the thick of the battle. They ran across the open grass toward the troupe running on foot and the line of vampires who fought alongside Arabella.

Several soulless leapt atop vampires and sunk teeth into their necks, chewing until blood spurt in every direction. The vampires flailed arms, some pulling the skeletons off and flinging them into the horde. Their fangs emerged, pupils swelling as they turned and staggered back toward the ward. Other vampires used their speed, running back and forth, sweeping the nearest line of the soulless back, but it didn't hold them for long. The movements were too fast for Nemera's eyes to track for long.

The enchantresses joined Arabella, swinging blades and unleashing their magic. Skeletons flew back, some flying in pieces back toward the crawling, hissing horde. But no matter how many times blades, magic, or fangs struck the soulless, they never tired, never slowed. They moved in pieces toward them, sinew pulling bones back together as they crawled along the ground.

There's no stopping them, Nemera realized.

If they couldn't be killed, the only option was to flee. They had to get to the ward and soon. More vampires fell, and the soulless descended upon them like insects, tearing them apart. Limbs flew before disintegrating into ash. This caused the undead to hiss, making them even more incensed as they clawed forward.

Nemera thought she saw flashes of movement before more

people staggered from Rowan's arms and flung themselves into the purple-blue magical barrier.

When Rowan disappeared again, Nemera watched in horror as another vampire was torn to shreds. Stomach turning, she fell to a knee. Had that been Rowan? Had he been trying to rescue another human and was overtaken?

The enchantresses and vampires were mere yards from the wall when the bulk of the troupe was before the ward and hurtling through it. But there were so many soulless that they blocked out the rising sun. It was like a hive of ants had ascended from their underground nest and climbed atop each other to form a dark wall. More of the soulless descended from the nearby forest.

As the troupe ran past Nemera and toward the open gate, tears streamed down some of their faces. Some fell over, retching, while others had massive gashes down their arms or across faces. All heaved gasping breaths.

Some enchantresses guided the troupe toward the wall, hurrying them to safety. None stopped to ask questions. They ran for all they were worth.

Then Arabella, the enchantresses, and the remaining vampires pushed through the ward. There were only five of the immortals.

Tears streamed down Nemera's cheeks as she felt the press of Rowan's arms. He'd appeared before her in a blur, and he clung to her so hard, it was painful.

"You're okay," she managed, her voice cracking. "You're okay."

Somehow, despite the odds stacked against them, he'd made it. He smelled of blood and sweat, and his arms were slick. But she clung to him, afraid that if she let go, she might never see him again.

He pressed a kiss to her forehead and a second, holding her tightly, before turning back to the ward.

It was then she looked up, and her eyes drew wide.

Darkness fell over them as a shadow blocked out the line of

sunlight on the horizon and extended over the open grass before the wall.

The soulless climbed atop each other atop the ward, uncaring as their bones cracked and steam rose into the air when their bodies touched the dome. As though they couldn't feel or didn't care that their bones were disintegrating at the contact. They hissed, a deep guttural sound, as they moved like insects atop each other. There were hundreds of them, climbing on top of each other until they blocked out the sky.

Then to her horror, the ward bent forward.

It reminded her of a piece of worn fabric that had stretched too far, under too much weight. It bulged at the top of the arch of the dome where dozens of the soulless had climbed. They fell into the groove, which only deepened it. The skeletal creatures fell ten feet toward the ground as the ward bent.

Nearby, the enchantresses stood in wordless horror as they stared at the demons.

"Is it supposed to do that?" Nemera said, her hands sweaty as she gripped Rowan's forearms where he held her.

He shook his head slowly as though uncertain what to say. Before he could respond, she heard Arabella's voice shout above the utter silent plains outside of the wall.

"Get back!"

Rowan scooped Nemera into his arms and was moving in an instant.

"Get behind the wall!" Arabella shouted, but her voice was lost in the screaming as the worst happened.

Where the ward bent forward, a tear appeared. It sounded like the ripping of parchment. At first, the hole was only a few feet wide, and a couple bones spilled through, falling onto the ground and writhing like a dying animal. Some shadowy sinew latched onto the bones, pulling them back together. Then the tear widened further, and hordes of the soulless spilled through.

The purple-blue hue of the ward flickered like a candle about to go out. And then demons were spilling onto the grass in the dozens.

Demons had broken through the ward.

It wasn't possible.

For Nemera's entire life, the ward had been the barrier between the demons and Shadowbank. It had been the shining beacon of the village, the very reason they could survive in this unforgiving land. But now, the demons had gotten through.

Shrieks of terror filled the air, drowning out the shouts of the enchantresses standing inside the ward. But Arabella, Jessamine, Brynne, Cora, and the others didn't turn for safety. Instead, they faced the oncoming horde.

"We have to help them!" Nemera shouted, but Rowan shook his head as he ran across the field toward the open gates.

"We have to trust the enchantresses now," he said. "They're our last hope."

As they passed through the gates and into the safety of the village, she heard the shout of the head enchantress from the wall above.

"Close the gates!"

Some of the troupe were still out there.

Nemera tried to push herself out of Rowan's arms as the gates closed. Screams were carried on the wind from the other side of the wall.

"We have to help!" she said, kicking and twisting, trying to get free.

But he ignored her, calling out, "She needs a healer!"

Guards ran across the streets, shouting orders, and archers ran up the stairs to the wall above. Those arrows would be useless against this kind of evil. There was no stopping creatures that couldn't die.

More enchantresses appeared, but these weren't warriors. They were the healers of the order.

In moments, Nemera was laid on the ground, and an enchantress kneeled over her. She tried insisting others needed to be healed first, but neither the healer nor Rowan listened to her. Her vision swirled as another wave of dizziness crashed into her, and she realized then how weak she truly was.

Something warm plunged into her as the enchantress' palms pressed against the center of her chest. It felt like wet electricity shot through the very marrow of her bones, and her entire body drew taut as a scream caught in her throat. Somewhere beneath her, she registered that Rowan held her head in his lap even as her arms scraped against the ground.

Liquid shot through her veins, and it felt like a dam had been torn down and a torrent was unleashed. It was as though the healer had convinced her body's blood to replenish itself in mere moments. The torrents swept through her body, filling her chest and then her limbs.

Strength flickered in her veins, and she was on her feet.

I have to help, she thought. *There are people out there.*

But she managed only a single step before her knees gave out. Rowan caught her, scooping her into his arms once more.

"Make sure she rests," the healer said somewhere behind her. "She'll be weak for days after what I just did."

Darkness filtered over Nemera's vision, and her eyes fluttered closed even as she willed herself to stay awake. As she faded from consciousness, she heard the hissing bellows of demons beyond the wall—and the responding shouts of the enchantresses.

Their last line of defense now that the ward was no longer enough to protect them.

Then she succumbed to the darkness.

Chapter Sixteen

ROWAN

Rowan faded in and out of sleep where he sat beside Nemera's bed, gripping one of her small hands between both of his. At some point, he must have rested his head atop the blankets because the next he knew, he was blinking awake.

The passing of the sun from one horizon to another had never seemed so long as it had the past two days that Nemera slept.

But he never left her side. He'd never leave her side again—thanks to her sacrifice that had given him his freedom. Hers and Arabella's sacrifice. He'd always be thankful for them both.

Nemera's chest rose and fell as she slept. She looked so peaceful.

Even with the healer's assurances that she was fine, that she just needed rest, worry filled him. Was she supposed to sleep this long? He feared she'd never come back to him, stuck in a state of slumber.

Hours later, Arabella came by the room and stood beside Rowan's chair.

She placed a hand on his shoulder and watched Nemera's sleeping form without a word. She was covered in bandages, scrapes, and bruises, and one of her eyes was swollen shut. But she was alive.

After some time passed, she said, "No one can know."

Slowly, he turned from Nemera to look at the enchantress, not releasing Nemera's hand.

"Know what?" he said. "That I'm a vampire or that there was a tear in the ward?"

Sighing, she dropped her hand from his shoulder. "Both."

He nodded, turning back to where Nemera slept.

"The other vampires are being granted passage by vessel as thanks for the part they played in saving the humans from the troupe," she said. "I'd tell you to join them, but..." She looked to Nemera's sleeping form. "I know you won't. So, if you're going to stay, the fewer people who know about your being a vampire, the safer you and Nemera will be."

"People would have seen me running too fast for a human and carrying the performers," he said. "Others might have seen me in the silver handcuffs."

"We're working to arrest the rest of the patrons from the House of Obscurities' private auctions," the enchantress said. "Hopefully, anyone who knows what you are will be behind bars soon. As for your running, I imagine most were focused on the horde."

"And the ward?" he asked. "I'm not the only one who saw it. Word is going to spread."

"It will," she agreed. "But we need to slow it for as long as possible."

Frowning, he turned back to the enchantress. "You're not surprised. You knew the ward was going to fail."

She ran a hand over her braid as she looked up at the ceiling. "I've been trying to fix it. I *will* fix it."

"That doesn't inspire confidence," he said carefully.

"I'm working on it," she said. "We stopped the horde before they went over the wall. That's what matters."

He paused, a thought occurring to him. "How do you kill the undead?"

A wicked smile lifted the corners of her lips. "We pushed demons back through the ward that's meant to keep them from going through."

They'd incinerated unkillable demons by forcing them through a barrier they couldn't pass through.

"A risky strategy," he said. "The ward could have torn again."

"It could have. But it didn't." Then she turned on a heel and patted his shoulder before heading for the door. "Tell Nemera I came by when she wakes."

"Enchantress," he began.

Arabella paused at the door, an eyebrow raised.

"Thank you," he said after a moment. "For coming after me."

She nodded her head. "Let's not make a habit of it."

A smile spread across his lips. "I wouldn't dream of it."

Then Arabella was gone, moving on near-silent feet, power rippling out from her as surely as the weight of responsibility she bore. He didn't agree with her choice to keep the ward's state secret from the people of Shadowbank, but he also understood that when word got out, it would cause panic.

And word would get out. It was only a matter of time.

Hours later, there was a shifting on the blankets, and he looked up from where he'd fallen asleep.

Nemera blinked, glancing around the room as she sat up in bed. "Where am I?"

Relief flooded his chest, the feeling so strong that for a moment, words were out of reach.

She was okay. She was back.

"The House of Obscurities," he said, wrapping his hands around hers even more tightly. "You've been asleep for two days."

He quickly brought Nemera up to speed about what had happened with the ward and Arabella stopping by. He'd learned that nearly a dozen enchantresses had died to stop the horde of the soulless from reaching the wall and that they'd repaired the ward. When Nemera heard this, she paled. For a moment, it reminded him of how pale she'd been on the plains only days earlier.

Rowan reached for a sealed scroll in his jacket that one of the staff of the House had given to him when he'd brought back an unconscious Nemera and they'd put them in one of the guest rooms.

She accepted the scroll from him. "What's this?"

He shrugged.

Breaking the seal, she unfurled it, scanning the contents. A minute later, she looked up, her brows furrowing.

"Trista left the House of Obscurities to me," she said, and tears welled in her eyes. "She must have known Jonas was going to kill her, and she'd prepared the documents before..."

Before she'd tried to help them and was killed for it.

Sadness filled him at not having a chance to get to know this female that clearly meant so much to Nemera—a female that had risked her life for theirs.

He watched her throat move as she swallowed and wiped her tears away.

"Where are the performers from the troupe?" she asked.

"The enchantresses are trying to find homes for everyone," he said.

"With your help, I'd like to hire them—the good ones, anyway. Not anyone who was loyal to Jonas." She placed the scroll back on the side table. "They will have a place to perform here."

He nodded. "I like the idea."

Then she grew strangely quiet, her voice barely above a whisper. "I'd like for you to stay, here. With me. If that's something you want, that is."

A smile as bright as the hope flaring in his chest broke out across his face. "I'd like that."

She bit her lip, her eyes flicking down to his lips and then back up to his eyes.

"There's something I have to tell you," she began, but Rowan had spoken at that same moment.

"I need to—" he began but stopped when she'd begun speaking.

They looked at each other, knowing smiles spreading across each of their faces.

"You go first," he said.

She bit the inside of her cheek. "In my marriage, I learned what love wasn't—and what it was I wanted from a partner. I learned that love isn't selfish. It comes in, invisible as the autumn winds, but as powerful as a storm. Love is kind and gentle. Love means wanting the best for another person. And I want to make your dreams come true, Rowan—whatever those are. I want to be by your side and help you achieve all your heart desires."

"I love you, too," Rowan said, smiling.

Her eyes rounded. "You love me?"

"I wanted to tell you the moment I left with Jonas," he said. "I love you with my entire being. I love you more than the air I breathe and more than the blood I crave. There is nothing I wouldn't do for you, nowhere I wouldn't follow you."

She bit her lip. "I love you, my vampire." Then her eyes grew distant before she added, "If you stay in Shadowbank with me, it could mean your death. We are living on borrowed time right now. There's a chance the ward could fall completely. And you'd have to hide what you are."

Slowly, he stood and leaned forward until his face was mere inches from hers. "It's worth it if I get to be with you. As for the ward, we must trust in Arabella to find a way to fix it."

She nodded. "In the meantime, we can make this place our home."

Home.

The word rumbled through his mind as he leaned forward and pressed a kiss to her lips. Desire blossomed deep within him, but he did his best to temper it. There would be time to learn every curve of her body, everything that made her lose control.

"You're my home, Nemera."
And it was the truth.

Epilogue
ROWAN

eeks later, Rowan stood behind the bar of the House of Obscurities, serving drinks to the humans in the packed common room. Nemera had disappeared around the corner into the larger adjacent room with the stage for the performers. Some squabble had broken out again, but it was all part of adjusting to their new life here. Soon enough, the former performers of Jonas' troupe would settle in.

When Nemera returned, her lips were pressed together in a straight line, and her hands fisted into the sides of her dress. She had filled out in recent weeks as he'd made sure she had both the time to rest and the food she needed to feel healthy and strong. And while she'd been beautiful before, something about seeing her thrive had him coming undone. Now, her bones no longer stood out in her chest. Instead, her breasts pressed against her dress' corset, which was deliciously low.

Not seeing him, she fixed her gaze on the ground and made several unladylike comments before she took a deep breath and her usual smile returned.

Unable to stop himself, he went over to her and pulled her into a hug. The feel of her beneath him, her warmth and realness, still took his breath away. As he held her, he allowed himself to nuzzle into her beautiful curls. She smelled of strawberries and sunshine. Her scent did something inside his chest.

Slowly, he took a step forward, forcing her to step backward until they were at the corner of the bar and in the shadows of a nearby storage closet. As she stepped backward, she tripped and began to fall, but he caught her and pressed her body between his and the wall.

"Rowan," she breathed. "What's gotten into you?"

"You." He nuzzled into her hair, enjoying the feel of her soft cheek against his. "I can't get enough of you."

She giggled, and the sound was like bells at dawn. "I'm working. We really should—"

He ran his tongue down the side of her neck to her collarbone. As he did, her words trailed off, and he could feel her body mold into his. Her hands ran up his chest, though she kept them above his shirt.

"I need you," he said, allowing his hips to thrust forward against hers. Allowing her to feel just how much he desired her.

She let out a soft moan.

"The closet," she gasped as her fingers curled into his shirt. "Now."

He scooped her off the ground and had them both inside the nearby storage closet in a moment, closing the door with a booted foot. There were brooms, mops, cleaning rags, crates of gods knew what, and barrels of their cheaper ale.

He wrapped her legs around his hips and pressed her back against the wall.

"Bite me," she said even as her hips rolled against him.

She was so eager.

Leaning forward, he ran his tongue down her neck again, enjoying the feel of her skin and the salty taste he'd left behind.

She shivered and laced her fingers through his hair.

"That's where this all started," he whispered into her neck between slow, sensual kisses. "A bite. In this place."

"I couldn't stop thinking about you after," she said as she

tilted her head back, allowing him greater access. "I couldn't help the way my body responded to you every time you were near."

"And how do you feel now?" he rumbled, nibbling at her neck with his teeth, avoiding his fangs as they lengthened.

"Like I'm being teased," she said.

"I'd never leave you wanting."

In a flash of movement, he moved one of his hands beneath her dress and ripped a hole in her undergarments. She gasped as he trailed his fingers along her cunt and then up to her clit.

"Is this what you wanted?"

"Yes," she moaned, thrusting her hips into his hand.

He still had so much to learn about sex and what it meant to be a good lover to her, but he wanted to spend every day learning how to do just that. If she wanted him. And damn him, there hadn't been a day that had gone by without their bodies tangling together and him losing himself inside her.

"And this?" he asked as he, at last, let his fangs out and sunk them into her neck.

She clapped a hand over her mouth as she cried out.

He pulled her blood into his mouth, savoring it. Everyone's blood tasted different. But hers reminded him of her scent that he loved so much. As he drank, he continued to move his fingers, stroking them against her clit in long up-and-down movements.

"Rowan," she rasped as she wrapped her arms around his neck. "I'm going to come if you keep touching me like that while..."

While he fed on her.

He didn't stop. He kept his movements at the same, steady pace, reveling at the wet softness of her beneath his fingers. *Fuck*, he wanted to bury himself inside of her, to feel her wetness all around him as he sheathed himself in her. But he was careful to drink slowly. After what had happened on the plains, he never wanted to lose control with her—never again.

"My breasts," she gasped. "Bite my breasts."

Gently, he removed his fangs from her neck, and she gave a

soft whimper. He allowed his gaze to move down her neck, to her collarbone, and down to the swell of her breasts.

Licking his lips, he said, "Untie your corset, or I might have to rip it off you. Then what will the patrons say when they see you like this? Fucked senseless by the staff."

Her hands left his neck, and she fumbled with the laces at her chest. After a moment, she untied the laces and pulled them loose. As she breathed, her breasts heaved, and he leaned forward, pulling one of her nipples into his mouth. He sucked and pulled until the little bud hardened before moving to the other breast and doing the same.

All the while, he never stopped moving his fingers inside of her.

When she made a noise that sounded like a plea, he peeled his lips back, allowing his fangs free once more, before sinking them into the soft flesh on either side of a nipple.

He'd never done that before, but he'd moved on instinct. And he was rewarded with the sound of Nemera's pleasure as she came. He plunged into her with his fingers, and her walls spasmed around him. With every pull of her blood, he felt his mind go hazy and his cock grow even harder.

Once her pleasure had subsided, he placed her on the ground before grabbing the laces at his britches. In a single movement, his cock was free, but he was otherwise dressed. She looked down at him, licking her lips.

"You want to be fucked in a closet, Nemera?" he asked as he closed the distance between them once more.

She didn't look at his eyes. Instead, her gaze was fixed on his erect cock.

"Yes."

He grabbed her legs and wrapped them around his hips once more. Then he sheathed himself inside of her.

"Like that?"

She dug her fingers into his shoulders, but he didn't care. He wanted to feel her nails raking against his skin.

"Fuck me, Rowan," she said. "Please. I want to feel you come inside me."

He thrust into her once, twice. She was so wet for him, and he moved without resistance.

"If we're going to do this, and I mean *really* do this, there's something you should know," he said. "Vampires can't have children. If that's something you want, then I may not be the right male for you..."

He allowed his words to trail off, uncertain what to say next.

Even as he was sheathed inside of her, their bodies joined, wanting nothing more than to be exactly where he was, he knew he had to tell her this. He wanted to be the one to give her the world, but he also knew there were things he couldn't give her.

To his surprise, she didn't pull away. Instead, she thrust into him as she said, "I don't want kids. I never have. This world is too cruel for me to want to bring more people into it." Leaning down, she pressed a soft kiss to his lips. The gesture was a stark contrast to the rougher thrusts she was urging him to do with her body with the way she moved her hips. "I want you, Rowan. Whatever time we have left on this earth, I want to spend it with you."

Tears filled his eyes, and he leaned forward, kissing her back.

"Now, stop talking, and fuck me," she said.

He did just that.

With one hand, he held her to him, pressing her back against the wall as he fucked her. With the other hand, he grabbed a fistful of her gorgeous curls and pulled, forcing her head back. While he made sure to be gentle, he also knew his little human liked to be fucked rough. Their weeks together had taught him as much. With her head tilted back, he leaned forward and sunk his fangs into her soft flesh once more.

Soon, they were both coming undone with each other's names on their lips.

They may not have long before the ward fell and the dark creatures of the forest were upon them. But he wanted to spend every moment with her. And should they come, he would fight to protect her.

She was his sun, and he was a planet pulled into her orbit. And he would follow her anywhere.

From now until eternity.

Thanks for reading Auctioned to the Vampire*!*

*Want to see what happens when Rowan gets the hots for Nemera when she's on her period? I wrote an **exclusive bonus scene** just for you! **Click here to download** (e-book only) or go to* ***bit.ly/ATTV-bonus-chapter***.

Click here** to read the first book in the Wild Shadows Series,* **Kissed by a Demon**, *or go to* ***bit.ly/KissedbyaDemon.

*If you'd like to be considered for an **advanced review copy (ARC)** of my future books, **please fill out this form** (e-book) or go to* ***bit.ly/ReadRosalynStirling***.

Acknowledgments

As ever, I'd like to thank my editors, beta readers, critique partners, proofreader, and cover designer for all their hard work to help me create this story. *Auctioned to the Vampire* wouldn't be what it is without the help of so many.

I'd also like to thank my dear friend and mentor, who recommended I write Nemera and Rowan's story, specifically. I had so many ideas for stories I could write as a prequel to *Kissed by a Demon*, and it was my amazing friend who was like, "NOPE. WRITE THIS."

To my family and loved ones, thank you for your continued support in encouraging me to write. I wouldn't have had the courage to be on this beautiful journey without you.

Lastly, I'd like to thank you, the reader, for reading this story. Stories only come alive in imaginations when there are people to enjoy it. I hope it was a fun read for you, and I'm so thankful you took a chance on my writing!

About the Author

Rosalyn Stirling is an author of steamy fantasy romance. In her free time, she enjoys reading and watching stories where love wins against all odds and the lovers find their happily ever after. She can be found at your nearest bookstore, tea in hand, dreaming of other worlds.

Want to stay up to date with everything Rosalyn is doing? Join her newsletter! You'll get first access to cover reveals, teasers, and giveaways.

bit.ly.com/RosalynStirlingNewsletter

Connect with her on social media:
Instagram (@rosalynstirling)
Facebook (Author Rosalyn Stirling)

www.ingramcontent.com/pod-product-compliance
Lightning Source LLC
Chambersburg PA
CBHW061542310726
48972CB00008B/2577